FEDERICO FELLINI

THE DREAM OF LIFE

Kate Fuglei

THE MENTORIS PROJECT

Mentoris Project
745 South Sierra Madre Drive
San Marino, CA 91108

Copyright © 2022 Mentoris Project

Cover design: Jim Villaflores

More information at www.mentorisproject.org

ISBN: 978-1-947431-44-7

Library of Congress Control Number: 2022931917

All net proceeds from the sale of this book will be donated to the Mentoris Project whose mission is to support educational initiatives that foster an appreciation of history and culture to encourage and inspire young people to create a stronger future.

Publisher's Cataloging-In-Publication Data
(Prepared by The Donohue Group, Inc.)

Names: Fuglei, Kate, author.
Title: The dream of life : a novel based on the life of Federico Fellini / Kate Fuglei.
Description: San Marino, CA : The Mentoris Project, [2022]
Identifiers: ISBN 9781947431447 (paperback) | ISBN 9781393755005 (ePub)
Subjects: LCSH: Fellini, Federico--Fiction. | Motion picture producers and direc-tors--Italy--History--20th century--Fiction. | Italy--In motion pictures--Fiction. | Imagination--Fiction. | LCGFT: Biographical fiction. | Historical fiction.
Classification: LCC PS3606.U39 D74 2022 (print) | LCC PS3606.U39 (ebook) | DDC 813/.6--dc23

The Mentoris Project is a series of novels and biographies about the lives of great men and women who have changed history through their contributions as scientists, inventors, explorers, thinkers, and creators. The Barbera Foundation sponsors this series in the hope that, like a mentor, each book will inspire the reader to discover how she or he can make a positive contribution to society.

Contents

Foreword   i

Chapter One: The Dream of Childhood   1

Chapter Two: The Dream of Nature   19

Chapter Three: The Dream of Rome   37

Chapter Four: The Dream of Reality   69

Chapter Five: The Dream of Directing   99

Chapter Six: The Dream of Redemption   121

Chapter Seven: The Dream of the Present   141

Chapter Eight: The Dream of Women   161

Chapter Nine: The Dream of Death   179

Chapter Ten: The Dream of History   193

Chapter Eleven: The Dream of Memory   205

Chapter Twelve: The Dream of Chaos   217

Chapter Thirteen: The Dream of the Future   227

About the Author   239

Foreword

First and foremost, Mentor was a person. We tend to think of the word *mentor* as a noun (a mentor) or a verb (to mentor), but there is a very human dimension embedded in the term. Mentor appears in Homer's *Odyssey* as the old friend entrusted to care for Odysseus's household and his son Telemachus during the Trojan War. When years pass and Telemachus sets out to search for his missing father, the goddess Athena assumes the form of Mentor to accompany him. The human being welcomes a human form for counsel. From its very origins, becoming a mentor is a transcendent act; it carries with it something of the holy.

The Mentoris Project sets out on an Athena-like mission: We hope the books that form this series will be an inspiration to all those who are seekers, to those of the twenty-first century who are on their own odysseys, trying to find enduring principles that will guide them to a spiritual home. The stories that comprise the series are all deeply human. These books dramatize the lives of great men and women whose stories bridge the ancient and the modern, taking many forms, just as Athena did, but always holding up a light for those living today.

Whether in novel form or traditional biography, these books

plumb the individual characters of our heroes' journeys. The power of storytelling has always been to envelop the reader in a vivid and continuous dream, and to forge a link with the subject. Our goal is for that link to guide the reader home with a new inspiration.

What is a mentor? A guide, a moral compass, an inspiration. A friend who points you toward true north. We hope that the Mentoris Project will become that friend, and it will help us all transcend our daily lives with something that can only be called holy.

—Robert J. Barbera, Founder, The Mentoris Project
—Ken LaZebnik, Founding Editor, The Mentoris Project

Chapter One

THE DREAM OF CHILDHOOD

Federico Fellini pulled away from his mother's grasp. He ran to touch the gigantic circus poster that hung on the side of the Arco d'Augusto in Rimini. He placed his tiny hands on the paper to see if the horse, the lady with the red feather who was winking at him, the leering clown, were real. It was his fourth birthday, January 20, 1924, and his father had promised him a trip to the circus. Circus and birthday aside, there was still marketing work to do.

Ida Fellini, Federico's mother, grabbed his hand and pulled him through the plaza at Mercato Atri and under the arch. They passed a Blackshirt parade. These parades now happened on all market days. The prime minister, Benito Mussolini—known as Il Duce—never let the citizens of Italy forget who controlled the government. The people of Rimini had now grown used to the parades. Federico ignored the drumbeats and the grim faces of the soldiers. Their monochrome movement faded into the background. He looked up at the colors of the posters. He was transfixed.

"Take my hand," said his mother. "Don't pull away again or you'll be swept up with the Blackshirts." Ida gripped Federico's hand so tightly his bones hurt.

Hours before, when they had gone to the market, the plaza they entered had been empty. Now it was filled with a huge yellow and red striped tent. Men sauntered about in striped shirts. They had muscles like ropes. Their porkpie hats were shoved on the back of their heads. They whistled as they affixed green flags to the top of the tent. The flags snapped in the sharp breeze off the Adriatic sea. Wagons circled the tent. The sides of the wagons were painted with horses flying through the air, women with blond ponytails straddled on top. Tiny white poodles cavorted around the edges of the wagons. They ran in circles, skipping and yapping, in and out of the tent flap, which was held open with polka-dot fabric.

"Please, Mamma, can we go inside? Just for a moment?"

Federico looked up at his mother with large brown eyes. His shock of dark curly hair stood up no matter how much pomade she used. He needed a father's touch. But his father was rarely home. Federico was always asking for something, always pushing the limits. Then he would crawl onto his mother's lap and give her the sweetest hugs and endearments. He was just like his father.

"I've got all this food from the market . . . and your brother is in the carriage," Ida said.

Indeed, Riccardo, who was two , looked up at Ida from his shaded carriage. The clock on the tower of the church indicated that the noon sun would be blazing soon.

"Riccardo is hungry and we need to get home before the heat of the day."

Federico snatched a pignoli cookie out of her string bag and stuffed it into his brother's mouth.

"He'll be fine, Mamma."

With that, Federico lifted the flap of the circus tent and rushed inside. Ida sighed. It was impossible to say no to Federico.

She stood, looking out at the gray waves of the Adriatic. They slapped against the pier that led out to the sea. She could see old men, stooped like question marks, casting their fishing lines. Their sons had gone out for the big catches before dawn.

She had a moment to herself for the first time that day. She wondered what in life had brought her to this provincial town. Rimini was not where she had dreamed of spending her life. She was lured there by Urbano Fellini. He was the handsome man who had swept her off her feet. She had been perfectly happy growing up in Rome, where she belonged. The Barbiani family was respected and sophisticated; they held Saturday soirées in their well-appointed apartment and strolled together on the via Veneto on Sundays, stopping to greet friends at the sidewalk caffès. Her parents were vehemently against her marriage to Urbano Fellini. They felt he was beneath her. She refused to listen.

Ida had a sense of dread the first night of her marriage to Urbano. He left the marriage bed to carouse with his pals. His sales job had brought them to Rimini, a town she hated. It was full of German and Swiss tourists in the summer. They descended like flies, taking over the tawdry caffès and shops. In the winter

Rimini was deserted. The women she met had nothing interesting to talk about; they were not educated, for the most part. Marketing, going to church, and raising their families took up their whole lives.

Urbano, who sold Parmesan cheese, olive oils, and other comestibles, was on the road most days of the week. He traveled around Emilia-Romagna, sometimes throughout Italy and a few times as far as France and Germany. Ida was left at home with a baby and a now-active toddler. Federico never stopped. He never napped, as other toddlers did, and even if Ida had been inclined to sit in courtyards gossiping with neighbor women, she was unable to as she was constantly watching Federico. When Urbano returned from his sales trips, there were frequent arguments that centered around his infidelity. When Ida found matchbook covers from nightclubs in distant towns and smelled perfume on her husband's shirts, there were loud confrontations.

Little Riccardo was an easy baby. Ida stared down at her younger son sleeping soundly in his carriage among the pounding and noise of a circus coming to town. The roustabouts, who seemed to be in no hurry, carried coils of rope and wiped their faces in the midday heat. Grease stained their handkerchiefs. They whistled at young girls walking by. Ida looked at her infant son and thought, *Are you going to be inscrutable like all men?* She stared idly at the flap of the tent and realized with a start that Federico had been gone for ten minutes. He was forever escaping her grasp.

Federico had indeed escaped his mother. The moment he entered the tent, he smelled sweat and hay. Someone was cooking sausages. The combination was intoxicating. He saw a woman half-dressed in a tattered lace slip. He had never seen his mother in anything but a dress. The woman hummed a tune as she washed a red tunic in a wooden bucket. A rickety ironing board stood next to her. A little girl with curly red hair, not much older than Federico, was pressing a striped jacket. A man lay on the ground next to them, lifting a barbell. He wore no shirt. He stopped, got up and sat on a bale of hay, and lit a cigarette.

There were circus wagons lined up as far as Federico's eyes could see. The outsides were painted in a riot of colors with fantastic scenes depicted: women on horseback, acrobats flying through the air, and lions leaping through flaming hoops. Federico peered inside one of the wagons and saw a zebra. His heart pounded with excitement.

The little red-haired girl came out from behind her ironing board and took his hand. She led him into a smaller tent. There was a dressing table surrounded by lighted bulbs. On top of the table were all kinds of sticks in a profusion of colors: red, purple, blue, and green. There were powders and pots of creamy paints. A voice spoke up and Federico jumped in surprise.

"I didn't mean to scare you, little fellow. Who has my little Annamaria brought? You aren't in the circus, are you?"

The man had kind eyes. He sat on a brown chair. The stuffing was peeking out, but he didn't seem to notice. He was reading a newspaper that he flipped down in order to gaze at Federico. His hair was uncombed and he yawned while he talked. Everyone here seemed to go around half dressed.

Federico soaked in the atmosphere. It was as though they had all just awakened. Although it was after noon and Federico and his family had been up for hours, these circus people were just beginning their day.

"My papà, Luigi, is the star of the show. He is the best clown in all of Italy," said the little girl, hopping onto her father's lap.

He laughed, ruffling her curls. "I wish my pay reflected that. She's the only one who seems to think so. But I'll take it."

Federico's mouth hung open. He had never seen a real clown, let alone met one in person. He had seen posters featuring clowns all over Rimini and dreamed of going to the circus for his birthday. He had begged his parents relentlessly for weeks before they gave in.

"We . . . we are coming tonight," said Federico.

"Well, now you are getting a preview of us in our underclothes, right?" he said, plucking the yellowed straps of his undershirt. He turned to Annamaria. "Darling, take him to see Sally. I need to speak to Giovanni. We weren't paid yesterday and there is nothing to eat."

Annamaria grabbed Federico's hand and they ducked out of the makeshift tent. He had a million questions, but before he could ask, she had led him to the wagon with the zebra. There was just room for the two of them to slide inside. There were two wooden buckets near the zebra's head. One seemed to be for food; the other was filled with water. The zebra stood very still.

"This is Sally. You can wash her if you like."

She showed Federico how to take a sponge, soak it with

water, and slowly, gently wipe it over the flanks and legs of the wondrous animal. Federico felt the zebra skin. It was soft and leathery, like the pouch in which his father kept his sales receipts. It was moist like the semolina bread his mother made when the dough was ready to be put into the oven.

"Go ahead. Wash her. I think she likes you," said Annamaria. She seemed to understand how magical the moment was for Federico.

Then they heard a scream. A piercing voice shredded the air.

"What have you done with my son, you lousy fools?"

Federico recognized his mother's voice. He dropped the sponge and ran toward the sound. He saw her standing next to Annamaria's father. Her head was inclined toward him and she shook her fist in his face.

Federico ran to her as fast as his stubby legs could carry him. They were soon surrounded by circus people, many of whom were wearing threadbare bathrobes. They regarded Ida with a combination of curiosity and amusement. Ida stared back at them with unbridled contempt. Federico pushed through the crowd and hugged his mother's waist. She clung to him as though he had been lost for weeks. Ida dragged him outside into the early afternoon sunshine of Rimini. Federico blinked his eyes as he was rushed down the street. Ida used one hand to pull her elder son toward home while the other pushed the baby carriage. A string bag full of that evening's dinner hung from the handle. Federico turned his head backward, toward the circus.

"Dirty and disgusting. Do you still want to go tonight after seeing that?" asked Ida.

"Oh yes, Mamma," said Federico, "yes. With all my heart."

"We wouldn't be going if your father hadn't wasted money on the tickets. He goes away for weeks, then comes back and spoils you rotten. I, for one, have already seen more than enough of those circus tramps."

Federico said nothing except a silent prayer that his father would come home in time, keep his word, and take him to the circus.

Six hours later Federico sat on his father's lap in the second row of the circus. He was so close he could reach out and touch Sally the zebra, the lion, the horses, the gymnasts who did backflips around the ring, the six tiny white dogs who jumped through hoops and hopped up and down miniature staircases, the four white steeds that galloped around the ring with girls standing astride their glossy coats. The girls were so beautiful Federico could hardly breathe. His father pinched him when one of them winked and snapped her whip at them. Did it really happen or did he just imagine it? She had platinum blond hair in a high ponytail. The red velvet costume she wore was that of a female gladiator. Federico thought the trim on her skirt must have been made of pure gold. Her lips were the color of rubies and the muscles in her arms rippled as she gripped the reins of the fast-moving creature. Federico thought he could see breath coming out of its nostrils.

Following the crowd at the end of the circus parade was the performer who got the most applause: the clown. He juggled two milk bottles, lost them in the crowd, and then "found" them as he walked around the ring. His face was painted white with a large red mouth outside his own; diamonds of purple were affixed to his forehead and above his eyebrows. He walked in a jiggly, unbalanced manner, tripping and doing somersaults to stand up again. A second clown walked after him, quiet and relatively dignified, almost an opposite. The first clown juggled a bottle to Federico and his father. As he leaned over to retrieve it, he said, directly into Federico's ear, "Welcome back home, little man. You belong with us."

The circus lasted for three hours. Federico sat on his father's lap the whole time. It was a rare evening for the Fellini family. They were all together. Ida and Urbano let themselves enjoy the evening despite Ida's earlier dismay. It was an uncharacteristically warm night for January , and they strolled back along the passage by the sea, which was crowded with tourists during the summer. Couples strolled hand in hand. Federico was happy. He saw that his parents were happy. The happiness didn't last.

Their home was near the train station. As they reached their front step, the sound of the train from Rome made its mournful whistle.

"If we lived in Rome instead of this backwater, we could take our children to see real art instead of this nonsense," said Ida. "The costumes were so tattered they could barely keep them on. Did you really enjoy that?"

"I certainly did," replied Urbano, "and so did your son. He knows a good thing when he sees it. I enjoyed it all immensely."

Ida sniffed. "Their costumes were all but falling off. And filthy."

"I thought they were beautiful," ventured Federico, "like princesses. Or queens."

"They were tramps this morning. And tramps tonight," concluded Ida. She turned to Urbano. "You should have been there hours ago." She sighed. "Now it's time for bed."

Federico thought of Luigi. He suddenly felt a deep sadness. He realized what he had seen in Luigi's eyes. He was alone. He was lonely, existing apart from the world of respectability. The world in which his parents moved and lived was a world apart from the circus. They had a family, a home, an existence surrounded by material things. Luigi had only his red-haired daughter Annamaria, a dressing table, his sticks of makeup, and whatever communion he had with his audience. Fleeting respectability—only the here and now. Whatever happened between Luigi and his audience. That was what he had. Feeling and reception, give and take.

Federico couldn't wait to go to bed. This was where he could close his eyes and dream. His dreams were where anything could happen, where there were no limits, no judgments, no parents interrupting. He closed his eyes. He saw girls leaping on horses, flying in the air. He saw zebras galloping. He saw clowns in pairs, as mirrors of one another. They all invited him to join them. He did flips and jumps, and instead of landing on earth, he flew high into the air over the coast of Rimini. He saw his town from the air: the four cathedrals; the train station with tracks that led all the way to Rome; the school he would soon attend; the leather maker who offered him scraps for his puppets. They were all waving to him. They were full of joy and seemed to want to share it with Federico. They had none of the anger and sourness he experienced at home. But he couldn't find a way to get down to them. Just as he was about to call out, he heard a voice saying, "Federico, time to get up. We have to be at mass in an hour."

Ida Fellini made her way to church with her two sons. She had seen her husband off on a business trip to Milan early that morning. It was a competitive business, he said, and selling properly required beautiful clothing and frequent travel. There were arguments over whether the trips were escape or necessity.

Ida knew he was unfaithful. She didn't know what to do about it. She poured her anxiety and concern into her children. If their father had a lack of morals, she would make sure her children were raised with the strictest standards. They attended mass with rigor and regularity. Next year Federico would begin elementary school. Ida wanted to instill her rules in him before he was exposed to those of other families. She regularly asked her priest to pray for her family and to make her husband more faithful.

On this breezy Sunday in the spring of 1924 , they walked toward their church. They passed a group of Blackshirts who were drilling a gaggle of adolescent boys. A banner with Mussolini's visage waved in the wind.

Federico stared at them with his round, intelligent eyes. He did not respond to them. His expression remained passive—so much so that the leader of the group noticed and walked up to Federico. Assuming the boy would be excited by the attention, the young soldier showed Federico how to do the stiff-armed salute. Federico simply stared at him. He refused. He remained stock-still, staring at the soldier, who now grew confused. He looked at Ida. Was there something wrong with this boy?

Then he became angry. He knelt down, grabbed Federico's arm, and forced it up. As the soldier did this, Federico let out a loud raspberry. He made the sound by sticking out his tongue and blowing through his lips, as he had seen Luigi the clown do at the circus. Then he threw back his head and laughed. The Blackshirt was outraged and humiliated.

"He doesn't know what he's doing," said Ida. "He's just a little boy and he wants to get to church."

The soldier looked at them as though he didn't believe Ida. Ida pulled her son down the sidewalk toward their church. Federico turned his head and stuck out his tongue.

Urbano needs to talk to his son, thought Ida. *This is what comes of having an absent father.*

Federico began school that fall. It was like most provincial schools in small cities in Italy. As his elementary years progressed, Federico found the learning rote, the teaching uninspired. He had no interest in the droning speeches of the nuns who taught. He had even less interest in the sports games the other children played at recess. Kicking a ball was boring. He didn't care whether it went into a goal or not and he failed to understand why it generated so much excitement. Physical activity, at least the sort usually attributed to young boys, was anathema to Federico. He especially hated swimming, which was something most boys his age in Rimini did frequently.

The nearness of the beach and the attraction of the tourist trade during the summer months drew Federico and his gang of friends toward the sea. The bright umbrellas, the caffès, and the gaggles of travelers brought Rimini to life. Anchoring it all was the Grand Hotel that stood like an elaborate pink and white wedding cake, beckoning the rich and privileged to step from their cars and up the grand marble staircase. The hotel was well guarded against any intrusions by ragamuffin locals. They could only stand across the street and admire the cream-colored coupes that pulled up the circular driveway and dispensed men in tuxedos who rushed to open the doors for women who wore white fur capes and satin gowns. Federico peered at the grandeur while his friends swam and played in the waves. He hated getting wet and was ashamed of his skinny body.

The greatest pleasure for Federico was to lose himself in comic books. His father brought them to Federico as gifts and his mother disapproved. She couldn't disapprove, however, of *Corriere dei Piccoli,* or *Corrierino* ("Little Courier"), for short. It was a weekly magazine specifically printed and distributed for Italian children. The brainchild of educator and journalist Paola Lombroso Carrara, it was created as a way to attract children to reading and educational pursuits. The pedagogical thrust was aimed at the thousands of Italian children who had little or no educational opportunities. It appealed to children from all walks of life, especially ones like Federico who appreciated the beauty of the illustrations and the excitement of the stories.

It was the fourth time that hour that Federico had clomped down the stairs to the front door of their apartment.

"Stop the clattering. You'll wake Maddalena," said Ida, nodding toward Federico's baby sister. Her eyes narrowed at him. "What are you up to?"

"I'm waiting for my *Corrierino* magazine. Today is the day it comes. I'm waiting for Little Nemo," he said, twirling around in a circle.

"And who is Little Nemo?" asked Ida as she folded Maddalena's diapers.

"Mamma, it's my magazine. From America. Remember? I asked for the subscription for my birthday."

"Oh yes, I remember. Don't ever tell your Papà. He wouldn't approve of a waste of money over colored pictures of silly things in a magazine."

"Mamma, they are beautiful! They are drawn by Mr. Winsor McCay from America. Little Nemo lays in his brass bed, but he has fantastical dreams. He goes everywhere. He has magic adventures. He is a hero! Winsor McCay makes me dream." Federico demonstrated by lying down on the carpet and closing his eyes. A beatific smile came over his face.

Ida gave his foot a little kick. "That may be what they do in America. But in Italy we tend to business. Get off the floor and behave yourself."

"Yes, Mamma," said Federico.

When he heard the postman's bell, he raced down the stairs and spent the rest of the afternoon poring over the magazine, dreaming of Little Nemo. Ida was too busy with Riccardo and Maddalena to notice.

Corrierino also reprinted the Katzenjammer Kids, a comic strip that detailed the adventures of two rambunctious brothers who loved to play tricks on their straight-laced mother; Felix the Cat, an enormous black feline with a perpetual grin; and Happy Hooligan, a hobo who encountered a good deal of misfortune but was never glum despite his low circumstance in life. Happy Hooligan significantly had two brothers, Gloomy Gus and snobby Montmorency, who were always unhappy despite their wealth. It was the founding notion of *Corrierino* to teach history, culture, and art through appealing, age-appropriate stories and beautiful illustrations. The magazines were printed with care to reproduce the vibrancy of the colors and details. None of it was lost on Federico.

He began to beg his mother for colored pencils, paper, and pens so that he could do his own drawings. Ida sighed and got them. It kept him out of her hair. She was happy to let Federico stay inside, reading comic books and drawing for hours at a time. When Urbano came home, he scolded his wife for making Federico into a "sissy." Urbano would then make noise about taking both boys to the park for some real exercise. They would sometimes go as far as digging out a deflated soccer ball. But usually by that time, Urbano had fallen asleep on the horsehair sofa in the living room. Federico would breathe a sigh of relief and pull out his drawings.

One warm Sunday afternoon in late May of 1926 , Urbano insisted, "We have a back garden. We pay for it but we never use it!" he bellowed. "Get the ball! I'm going to teach you to kick a ball."

They lumbered out to the back garden. It was still and hot. Urbano dropped the soccer ball and kicked it toward Federico.

"Now kick it back! No, don't let it go through your skinny legs."

The ball had rolled to the back of the garden, by their fence. A neighbor with blond hair appeared and smiled over the fence at Urbano. Urbano forgot soccer and went to talk to her.

"Go find the ball, Federico."

As Federico reached the end of the garden and parted the ivy that clung thickly to the walls, he noticed a small door. He had never seen it before. He heard music. It sounded like an accordion. The same notes were being played over and over again. There was a rusted handle on the door and Federico turned it. It opened with a creak. A shower of crusted mud and dead ivy fell on his head. Federico wiped his eyes and stepped outside the door.

Across the stone-covered alleyway was an open archway. Inside the archway was a raised wooden platform. On it sat a man dressed in a red silk robe. There was a music stand in front of him and he held an accordion on his lap. His large, fleshy face glistened with sweat. He grinned at Federico and beckoned him inside.

"The back door to the theater isn't usually open. But it's so hot. We want to air it out before tonight's show."

Federico wandered into the dark theater. His eyes grew accustomed to the darkness as the musician gave him a hand. He stepped up onto the platform. He was in the middle of a small stage. There was one lightbulb on a stand in the middle of the platform.

"It's the ghost light," said the musician, referring to the single bulb. "It is to appease the ghosts of the theater, to give them a place to dance and sing and perform so that they will let us do so. You know what *appease* means, little man? It means to make happy. That's what we artists do. We see the pain in life. We show it to people. Then we take it away. We make people happy. That's our job. That's what we get paid for."

Federico heard his father's voice calling him.

"I have to go," said Federico.

"You'll be back, though, right?" said the man. He played a short riff on his accordion.

Federico shook his head vigorously up and down. "Yes!" he said. "Oh yes!"

He ran out of the musky darkness and into the searing afternoon sun. A jolly tune rang out from the accordion and he skipped to the beat. He said nothing to his father, who had already forgotten about soccer. Federico instinctively knew his mother would not like theater people. So he kept it a secret. He vowed to visit again.

That night, he dreamed he was a puppet master. All the

people in his life—his mother, his father, his brother, his little sister, the boys who teased him about being skinny, the man with the accordion—they were all puppets on strings. And he, Federico, stood above them, controlling their every move.

Chapter Two

THE DREAM OF NATURE

The rain came down in sheets in Rimini. It was a Saturday night in March, 1925, and a light mist had turned to a sunset downpour. The crowds at the Fulgor cinema were crushed together under the marquee waiting for the doors to open. Electric bulbs outlined the posters that advertised the feature for that evening. Federico was holding his father's hand. He couldn't see anything but pant legs and the stockings and pumps of women dressed in their Saturday best. He had begged his parents to take him along to see his first film.

The rain let up and the crowds parted just enough for Federico to see a woman dressed in a skintight white frock. She wore a red beret cocked at a jaunty angle on her head. Her brown curls were carefully coiffed. She was standing directly under the poster for *Maciste all'inferno,* the feature they were about to see. The light shone down on her, giving her an unearthly glow. She removed her fur wrap, revealing a curvaceous figure, and bent to fix the seam in her stocking. She drew appreciative glances from every man in the crowd. Several offered to help her remove any mud that might have splashed on her legs from the rain. Wives elbowed their husbands, Ida among them. She pulled her husband and son into the cinema.

Federico looked back at the woman, and as he did, his father bent down to say to him, "She is Gradisca. Now that's what I call a *real* woman."

He didn't know exactly what his father meant, but he knew there was magic in the moment. He filed it away for dream material.

Federico knew it was special for a five-year-old to be in the Fulgor cinema on a Saturday night. He understood intrinsically the decorum he should follow: no talking, no begging for treats from the ice cream seller or the candy lady who hawked their wares to a welcoming crowd before the film started. Federico sat quietly on his father's lap. He didn't move a muscle. They had jostled into the theater and had stood for a moment until Ida pushed their way onto a wooden bench. Federico could smell wet wool and a sweet, spicy mix of perfumes. Above him, gold nymphs were painted on the ceiling. The walls were hung with red silk.

As the lights went down, his father said, "Maciste is the world's strongest man. He can do anything. Anything. He can conquer death, enemies, fire, and now he is going to conquer hell itself."

"He is going to go to sleep," said Ida. "Federico doesn't care about Maciste in hell. He's five years old."

The film opened on the river of Acheron with the devils of hell making their way to earth to tempt Maciste.

"The powers of evil are visiting earth," Urbano whispered to Federico.

Federico's eyes were as wide as saucers. He gripped his father's hand as the apostles of the devil stood looking over the earth, pitchforks in hand. Once Maciste descended into the fires of hell, Federico was as terrified as he had ever been. But he couldn't look away. There were devil orgies, devils flying through the air, devils beating drums, devils surrounding Maciste, dancing girls whose kiss meant eternal damnation tempting Maciste, headless devils trying to draw him into the fiery abyss of hell. Struggling between fear and temptation, Maciste is lashed, Christlike, to a cross, condemned to fiery limbo, until a child on earth on Christmas Eve prays for him. Maciste is saved from certain hell.

When the lights went up, Federico couldn't move. He sat in a trance. He seemed to be asleep with his eyes open. He held his parents' hands as they made their way down Corso d'Augusto to their home near the train station.

"I told you we shouldn't have taken him to see that," said Ida, putting her hands over Federico's ears. "It frightened him."

Federico turned on his parents. He drew himself up to his full five-year-old height and spoke to them loudly and forcefully.

"I was NOT frightened. I was Maciste and Maciste was me," he proclaimed.

His parents were startled. It was such an odd thing for a child to say that even the Saturday night revelers who filled the sidewalks stopped and looked. Ida and Urbano reached for their son's hand, but he stalked ahead of them all the way home.

Federico fell asleep that night hearing the last train from

Rome enter the nearby station. Its mournful whistle reminded him of Maciste's fiery abyss. He dreamed he was Maciste, fending off the powerful devils but giving in to the temptations of the dancing girls, who all began to look like Gradisca. He snatched the pitchforks of the devils and snapped them in two with his strong arms, all the while protecting dancing girls from eternal damnation. The dream took him from the red fires of hell to the blue of the sky and white puffy clouds; he was a baby being rocked by Gradisca and fanned by dancing girls in golden breast-plates. Then Ida's voice cut through his bliss. It was time to go to Sunday mass.

Throughout Federico's childhood he begged to go to the Fulgor cinema as often as possible. There were other fancier cinemas in Rimini, but the Fulgor was the one that drew the local crowd: the workmen who looked forward to their Saturday night out; the teenagers who used the darkness to kiss their dates; the children who sat, entranced, as they entered worlds they had never before known. Federico loved walking down the Corso d'Augusto and seeing the vivid, colorful posters advertising Paul Muni as Scarface, Mae West in seductive poses, and the Marx Brothers with their explosion of anarchy. Even Ida had to laugh at the antics of W. C. Fields. They all swooned at the dancing of Fred and Ginger. The crowds at the Fulgor were riveted by the worlds to which cinema exposed them; America was for them a place where gangsters ruled, madcap comedians amused, and romantic couples danced the night away. They forgot their aching backs, sore fingers, and the problem of putting food on the table. They forgot, for a few hours, the darkening clouds of repression in the faces of the Blackshirts who patrolled their streets, the changes that were being wrought by Fascism.

The movement of the swaying train thrilled ten-year-old Federico. The villages, farms, and the patchwork quilt of crops all passed by like a living comic strip. The whole Fellini family was traveling together—Urbano and Ida and their children, Federico, Riccardo, and Maddalena. They were packed into a compartment alongside an old man who munched on a sausage. A woman dressed head to toe in black sat next to him. The man kept offering her bites of the sausage even though she shook her head no each time. Her horrified looks never seemed to deter him.

They fascinated Federico. All humans seemed to have this effect on him. He was endlessly curious about his fellow human beings and never seemed to tire of observing them.

"Federico, stop staring," whispered Ida, poking him.

He laughed and turned to look out the window. There was so much to see. The family was traveling to Rome to see Ida's uncle. Ida had received word that he was fatally ill. Respects had to be paid even though there had been an estrangement over her marriage to Urbano. A beloved relative was near death. It had been nearly ten years since Ida had seen them, but they were still family.

As the train pulled into the station in Rome, passengers began gathering their belongings. Federico gazed out the window. He had never seen such movement, such color, so many crowds of people all pushed together, all hurrying somewhere.

There were fruit sellers, balloon vendors, pushcarts with candy and newspapers, couples kissing passionately as they said hello. Or was it goodbye? Federico couldn't tell. There were luggage carts with children running along beside them. Posters adorned the walls of the station advertising cigarettes, liquor, and lipstick. It was impossible for Federico to look away from them. Then he realized the train car was empty. Porters were cleaning up for the next passengers.

Federico scrambled to catch up to his family. They rode in a cab to the Barbiani apartment. Ida maintained a grim silence while Urbano kept up a travelogue as they passed sights Federico had only seen in pictures. The Tiber River was on their left as they made their way along a crowded thoroughfare. The streets were teeming with people.

Urbano exclaimed about the ubiquitous presence of Blackshirts. The symbol of Fascism—the chaff of wheat with the hammer and sickle—was everywhere: on streetlamps, on signs, and on every government building. They drove down the new via dei Fiori that had been chiseled out as part of the modernization plan begun by Mussolini. The Barbiani apartment was not far from the Fascist headquarters, a large square building with a stone edifice on which the visage of Mussolini hung. It filled the once-pleasant plaza in front with a bleak reminder of the current occupant.

Rome was a profusion of movement, color, and human endeavor. As they rounded a corner, the Coliseum, with its massive stone layers, appeared. To Federico, it looked as though a giant bite had been taken out of it.

Riccardo was asleep and Maddalena was fussing as they drove up the steep stone street to the Barbiani home. They slowly climbed the marble steps and greeted Ida's parents, who were restrained but delighted to see their grandchildren for the first time. Tears rolled down Ida's mother's cheeks as she hugged them. She and her husband stiffly acknowledged Urbano, whose discomfort at being there was barely disguised.

They were led to a small bedroom at the back of the apartment, where Ida's Uncle Dom lay. He was an elderly man with a huge head and bright eyes, despite being bedridden. He beckoned to Federico immediately and put his large hand on his nephew's head.

"Why have I never met this fine young man?"

The question hung awkwardly in the air.

"Because I live in Rimini, sir," said Federico, bridging the silence.

"I suppose there are Fascists there, too. Those devils are everywhere now," said Ida's uncle, shaking his head and coughing.

"Don't listen to my brother-in-law," said Federico's grandfather with a scowl. "They are rebuilding a new Italy! The Fascists are doing great things. The road on which you drove here was carved out by Il Duce. He is finally draining the swamp outside this city, something no leader has been able to do. He is building new villages and towns—"

"He is a thug," Uncle Dom interrupted. "He has murdered thousands of people. He plans to take us to war again for no reason. He is anti-Semitic—"

"He is educating our children," said Grandfather. He was beginning to turn red in the face.

"Turning them into mindless Blackshirts!" screamed Uncle Dom.

"Stop it! Stop it, both of you!" yelled Grandmother. "They haven't even put down their bags yet and here you are arguing."

Ida led the two younger children and Urbano to a small room with a double bed and cots. Federico was given a tiny room almost the size of a pantry. He put down his bag of art supplies, which he now always carried, and opened the room's small window. It hadn't been opened in a long time and chunks of rust fell from the casement. He knelt on the bed and peered out. Federico gasped with pleasure.

Beyond the green plane trees of Hero's Park, he could see the massive dome of St. Peter's. The Garibaldi Monument, erected for the partisans who died trying to save the Roman Republic in 1849, stood in the foreground. Urbano had told Federico that a cannon was fired every day beneath the statue to commemorate their bravery. A breeze stirred the trees and they bent forward as if they, and all of Rome, were beckoning to Federico. The whole of Rome seemed to be laid out for Federico, framed by the tiny window.

He lay on his narrow bed and dreamed of flying over the beautiful city. Federico had heard of people falling in love with one another. He wondered if it was possible to fall in love with a city. He felt he belonged in Rome. Although he had only been in the city for four hours, he felt connected to its ancient mystery, to the pulse of its humanity, the possibility in its spiritual splendor.

As the family settled in for a weeklong visit, Federico spent time by Uncle Dom's bedside. The old man was at the end of his life, but he seemed to be revived by Federico and the young boy's interest in everything. Uncle Dom told Federico about the founding of Rome, and Romulus and Remus, who were suckled by a she-wolf. He claimed the family was directly descended from the Trojan War hero Aeneas.

Urbano snorted at all this and proposed escaping to the streets of Trastevere, the lively neighborhood that surrounded the Barbiani apartment. Federico, eager to explore Rome, begged to go along.

He walked with his father down the cobbled streets until they came to a local caffé and bar. Someone was playing a swing tune, "A Mori," and Urbano bent down, gave Federico a handful of money, and said, "Explore a little, kid. For an hour or so."

Nothing so wonderful had ever happened to Federico. He walked down the street stuffing the money into his pocket. He stopped for a gelato. Couples strolled arm in arm; they laughed and entered the caffès that dotted the street. Federico looked up. Laundry hung on lines, crisscrossing the street like so many kites. A woman leaned her hand on her cheek, saw Federico looking up, and scattered geranium petals; they floated down and fell at his feet.

He saw a sign for a puppet theater. It hung on a small door that was painted red. The doorway led to a brick path with a curtain at the end. A man with round black glasses and a huge grin ushered Federico into the theater space. It was like walking inside a jewel box. The walls were covered with blue velvet.

The show started, announcing the puppets of Vittorio Podrecca. Two marionettes representing Romulus and Remus battled it out on the miniature stage. A combination of puppets and marionettes created the tale of Cinderella, then Dante's *Inferno.* A small trio of live musicians played. The sets behind the puppets alternately depicted ancient Rome, Cinderella's palace, and the fires of hell. For a finale, a small puppet with a large bosom sang Gounod's "Funeral March of a Marionette."

When the lights went up, Federico sat, transfixed. He couldn't move. Suddenly he realized he had been there for nearly three hours. He jumped up, pumped the hand of Vittorio Podrecca, exclaimed that he would be back, and ran out into the Roman evening.

The atmosphere on the street was much more lively. It was the shank of the evening. Federico ran to the caffè where he had last seen his father. Urbano was seated on a barstool with his back to Federico. His arm was around the bare shoulders of a young woman who was laughing uproariously. Federico knew his father would not want to be interrupted. He waited until the young lady excused herself to go to the powder room. He ran inside and pulled his father, who was quite inebriated, out of the caffè and toward the Barbiani apartment.

"You're no fun," said Urbano, doing a jig, "no fun at all."

Federico bought his father an espresso. By the time they

reached the apartment, they were ready for the barrage of anger from Ida.

On the last day in Rome, Federico drew a picture for Uncle Dom. It was the view from his window with angels floating above. He gave it to Uncle Dom, who was duly impressed.

"You are an artist. I should have known. Don't ever let anyone tell you what to do. Not Mussolini, not the church, no one. You hear?" He kissed his nephew's forehead. "Now forget about me and go and live your life . . . live your life. It's the only one you've got."

"I will never forget about you," said Federico.

Two weeks later, a large wooden box arrived. It was from Uncle Dom in Rome and it was addressed to Federico. Inside was a puppet theater. It was almost as tall as Federico. It was complete with curtains, sliding doors for set changes, and a series of rods and winches for manipulating marionettes. It came with a note from Uncle Dom: *Follow your dreams.*

Federico went to work immediately, creating puppet heads from clay he borrowed from a neighborhood potter. A leather maker in Rimini gave him scraps for costumes. He spent hours recreating what he had seen in Rome. Ida was thrilled, as it kept her son from aimlessly roaming the streets with his pal Titta Benzi and other friends. Urbano, who spent less and less time at home, was shocked to find a fully formed puppet theater, complete with commedia dell'arte characters and scripted stories, in the middle of his living room.

For his part, Federico lost himself in the world of the

puppet theater. The real world fell away: the Blackshirts, the self-consciousness about his growing body, the boredom and sameness of the nightly strolls up and down from the caffès to the beach and back again. On nights when he joined friends wandering the streets of Rimini, they visited Saranghina, the rumba-dancing lady who lived on the beach, and Gradisca, the beauty of the Fulgor cinema. They played tricks on unsuspecting German tourists. They acted out scenes from Homer's *Odyssey* on the Plaza d'Novo, with Federico assaying the role of the wandering Odysseus. They jumped and cavorted, stabbing one another with fake swords and causing tourists to run in fear.

Rimini was two towns, in reality: the crowds of summer and the boredom of winter. But whatever the season, Federico's real pleasure came when he could lose himself in the magic of drawing or creating whole worlds in the puppet theater.

At the beginning of the summer of 1933, when Federico was thirteen years old, every adolescent boy in Rimini was sent to Balilla, the Fascist youth summer camp. Balilla was the nickname of Giovan Battista Perasso, the Genovese boy who, legend stated, started a revolt against Hapsburg forces in 1746. The Balilla camp's express purpose was to train young men for future assignments in the military. Balilla eschewed the traditions of Greek and Latin education and focused on physical strength and obedience to the Fascist philosophies.

Federico was able to attend the camp with his best friend, Titta Benzi. They had met in grammar school. Titta was blond, physically confident, and constantly merry. It was Titta who encouraged Federico and his friends to walk naked up to lovers on the beaches of Rimini and ask the time of day. It was Titta who devised a plan for stealing from the alms box. He was popular with females and had no problem flirting with flocks of feminine summer visitors.

Titta's family was also lively. Multiple generations lived under the Benzi roof, but there was always room for one more around their dinner table. They adopted Federico as one of their own. Titta's father was a virulent anti-Fascist. When the captain of the local Fascist squad found out that he was prohibiting Titta from attending Balilla, Titta's father was brought to headquarters. They forced him to drink castor oil until he soiled himself, then they threw him out onto the street. After that, Titta went to Balilla.

Dressed in black shirts, black fezzes, and green wool trousers, the boys were made to live in tents in the summer heat. Most of the day was spent doing physical exercise and marching. Federico despised every moment. Then he found out that there was a camp newsletter. He had brought along his art supplies. Titta encouraged Federico to offer up his talents.

The editor of the newsletter was a squat young man with an imperious air. He took a cursory look at some of Federico's work and said, "We need a drawing of the camp commander, not a comic strip."

Federico assured him he could do this. He hid his disdain with an obsequious manner: "I think I can."

The camp commander was a bald man with an alcoholic's veined, bulbous nose and thick, bushy eyebrows.

Federico's rendering was an exact likeness with just a hint of caricature. The editor didn't have the humor to see the exaggeration.

"This is very good. Quite good," he said.

It became Federico's first widely published drawing. The adolescents in the camp recognized that it made fun of its subject. Federico garnered a fair amount of notoriety for it. He reveled in the amusement and enjoyment it gave to the campers, who uniformly guffawed when they saw it.

Federico maintained an innocent stance when asked about it: "It is a respectful rendering of our beloved leader." His dark eyes were wide and innocent; the only giveaway was the twinkle.

Federico, Titta, and their friends spent the rest of their summer days and nights walking along the avenue that went from Raoul's Caffè, the smoky hangout of the locals, to the beach and back again. Federico befriended the owner of the Fulgor, a man who sported a thin mustache and wore a trench coat thrown over his shoulders; he had a passing resemblance to suave movie star Ronald Colman and used every opportunity to take advantage of his position. He hired Federico to create posters and caricatures of the stars in coming attractions. In lieu of pay, he allowed Federico to come to the Fulgor as often as he liked.

Federico eventually opened up a small art shop with Demos Bonini, an older artist who became a friend. The shop was across from the largest cathedral in Rimini and Federico often walked inside its cool marble interior. Tourists and the ladies of Rimini were patrons of the shop, which the two artists called Febo. Federico drew the portraits and Bonini colored them.

Gambettola, the farm on which Urbano grew up, provided an utterly different experience for Federico and Riccardo, who often visited there in the summers of their youth. Urbano's mother ruled their farm with an iron hand and was generous with her laborers. They repaid her with loyalty and friendship. Every summer Federico and Riccardo were welcomed to the large stone kitchen of their paternal grandmother, filled with farm workers and village friends from the local communities. In contrast to the tension of the house in Rimini, Gambettola was filled with warmth. Federico and Riccardo were given the freedom to roam the fields and pastures. Federico spent his time talking to the field workers, pig castrators, iron mongers, and mattress makers. He came to know about the lives of people who inhabited a world nearly untouched by modernization. Gambettola and similar villages represented the last gasp of worlds that had existed in the same way for centuries.

Itinerant workers went from village to village, as did traveling entertainers and tribes of gypsies, or Roma. Federico and Riccardo came upon their encampments every summer. Riccardo was frightened of their wagons, the smell of their cooking, and the manner in which they insinuated themselves into the community. Federico was fascinated by them; he was drawn to hearing about ancient hexes and curses, the stories they told by firelight. The traveling magic shows, fire eaters, jugglers, and troubadours who went from town to town entertaining at weddings and festivals brought laughter and joy to the isolated villages. Federico watched as they laid out their talents to the townspeople and then packed up for the lonely, dusty road.

~

In 1938, Federico Fellini was eighteen years old. He had graduated—barely—from high school. He had no interest in academia, although Urbano insisted that he get a law degree. Federico had fallen in love with a neighbor girl, Biancina. He saw her in the window of her apartment and began writing notes that Biancina returned with equal fervor. They began to meet secretly, with Federico stealing delicious cheeses and olives from his father's best stash. They met under the Arch d'Augusto and Federico rode with Biancina on his handlebars. They had picnics on the beach. Then Federico made the mistake of telling Ida about Biancina. All hell broke loose when Ida marched to the neighbors to let them know their daughter was being courted by a boy they didn't know. The affair was ended and Federico was heartbroken.

Federico found solace with Titta and his friends Molinari and Luigi Dolce. They walked to one of their favorite places in Rimini—the cemetery. They admired the arduous work of the gravediggers and, most of all, the singing of the beautiful young blond peasant woman whose job was to care for the gravesites. She was unfailingly cheerful and she skipped among the gravestones, placing flowers and wiping the granite with great care.

Untouched as the boys were by death, they found humor in the photographs on the gravestones and imitated the stern visages. They saw the names of their ancestors represented: Fellini and Benzi and Molinari and Dolce.

They left the cemetery and began a walk to the beach.

"What is it that you want out of life? What do you want to give to it? Get from it?" asked Federico.

Titta was surprised by his question. "My only fantasy is this, my only dream: a bare-naked lady, a bottle of wine, and a soft bed. That is my only desire. I don't need anything else."

"Really? You have no other ambition?" asked Federico.

"You are too serious tonight. Let's go to Raoul's and forget it. There will be other Biancinas. The sea is full of fish, my friend."

"Do you remember when the sea monster crashed up on the shore in Rimini?" said Federico.

"Who could forget it? Everyone was there," said Titta.

"What did it all mean?" asked Federico.

"What did what all mean?"

"Our childhood, this place, this town, the sea . . . ."

"Nothing. It all means nothing. Don't become a philosopher, my friend. It doesn't suit you. We are from Rimini. In Emilia-Romagna . . . we are simple people. We just live. There is no meaning."

They had reached the sea. It was January just before sunset and a gray mist was rising from the waves. Federico felt an ocean of loneliness and emptiness rise within him. He tried to remember a time when he had not felt that way. It was when he was in Rome, looking out the window, seeing the green trees swaying in the breeze, the dome of St. Peter's rising in the distance. There was promise and potential in Rome.

He turned to his friend. The breeze was blowing his blond hair straight back from his face and he could suddenly imagine Titta as an old, bald man. Titta would stay here, in Rimini; his life would be circumscribed by the walk from Piazza Cavour to Piazza Giulio Cesare. The people Titta knew now would be the people who would share his place in the cemetery.

Titta was wrong. There was meaning to life. The meaning of life was what we chose to give, those things to which we dedicated ourselves.

Federico decided at that moment that his life would have meaning—endless meaning and purpose. But to do so, he had to leave Rimini.

Federico informed his parents that he was going to Rome. He promised his father that he would most certainly attend the University of Rome with the intention of becoming a lawyer.

Ida saw her chance for escape. She declared that it was not suitable for a young boy to live by himself in Rome. She would follow him there and take Maddalena, too.

Federico's final night in Rimini was an all-night revel with Titta and friends. They closed down Raoul's, danced with Saranghina on the sand, and stood on the pier at dawn.

Titta could not let go of Federico. The two friends took the train together as far as Bologna, when the conductor realized Titta had no ticket. Now kicked off the train, Titta stood on the platform waving to Federico. As the train pulled out of the station toward Rome, Titta said something, but Federico couldn't hear it. He imagined Titta was saying, "You'll be back."

Federico never set foot inside the University or Rome or any other university. He arrived in Rome, the city that he loved, and although he hardly knew anyone, he was never alone or empty again.

Chapter Three

THE DREAM OF ROME

Federico splashed his face with water from the fountain in the center of the Piazza di San Giovanni. He took out a handkerchief to wipe away the droplets. He didn't notice a piece of paper fall from his pocket. He leaned against the cool stone of the fountain and looked out at the sun coming up over the top of the Egyptian obelisk that stood in the northwest corner of the square. He couldn't decide which time of the day in Rome he loved the most—this time, when the new day was dawning and the possibilities were endless, or the dead of night, when the unexpected appeared around every corner. It was all magical to him.

Piazza di San Giovanni was empty except for a pair of ancient women, dressed in black from head to toe, who brandished their brooms like weapons. They had fashioned the brooms with wooden handles to which they had attached boar's bristles. They attacked the dirt and trash in the square with a ferocity that belied their age. They were cleaning up after the Notte delle Streghe festival, a yearly event particular to this neighborhood.

Federico watched them and thought, *There is always something wonderful going on in Rome, around every corner, in every nook and cranny, down every alleyway.*

The night before, Federico had happened upon the festival, which took place each June 23. The revelry, begun in ancient times, was an attempt to scare away the ghost of Herodias, wife of Herod Antipas, who convinced her husband to decapitate John the Baptist. Now it was an excuse to celebrate and let loose. One ice cream vendor, explaining the reason for the festival, said to Federico, "See what happens when you marry the wrong woman? Stay single—that's my advice, young man. Play the field."

Fireworks, rattles, dancing, and drinking were at their height when Federico had come upon the square. He was there to meet his new landlady. His apartment, a tiny room with a bed and a dresser, was just off Piazza di San Giovanni. He took the festival and its revels as a good sign, a welcome to the neighborhood.

One of the cleaning ladies poked him with the bristle of her broom. "Is this yours, young man?" She held up a piece of paper.

Federico recognized it with a start. It was his first paycheck from *Marc'Aurelio,* the magazine that had hired him as a writer. The money was his first month's rent. Full of gratitude, he dug in his pocket for a tip.

The woman refused it firmly, saying, "I found it on the other side of the piazza, where the wind blew it." She pointed to the statue of St. Francis that held his arms up, reaching toward the sky. "He was looking out for you."

She gestured toward the Basilica di San Giovanni in Laterano. "Go inside. Pray. That's all I ask of you."

The woman walked away and began attacking the dirt with her broom. Then she stopped and turned toward Federico again. "You look like you need a mamma to care for you."

Federico sat back on the edge of the fountain. A mamma was just what he didn't need. Ida had moved to Rome with Federico's little sister, Maddalena, hoping to control her eldest son. She also wanted to take up the life she had left behind when she married Urbano and moved to Rimini. Ida saw this as a golden opportunity to escape the boredom of Rimini and the tensions of a troubled marriage. But she was no longer a young girl on the brink of life. She was now a middle-aged woman used to the relative peace and quiet of Rimini. Despite her husband's unfaithfulness, Ida was accustomed to the routines of marriage to Urbano. Old friends from her youth in Rome had either moved away or found new lives. Money was tight. There was nothing extra for going to the opera or the theater. The changes wrought by the Fascist regime brought new construction and restrictions to Roman life. Everywhere there was talk of a coming war. The life she had hoped to resume seemed to have disappeared along with her husband's hopes for a son who would be a lawyer.

Ida had promised her husband that she would see to it that Federico attended law school. So far, he hadn't set foot inside the University of Rome or any other institution of higher learning. Instead, the moment they arrived in Rome, Federico began to spend endless nights in caffès, making money by drawing portraits of patrons. She had no control over where he went and what he did. To make matters worse, her younger son, Riccardo, had joined them in Rome and claimed that he was going to be a singer, of all things. Ida was constantly furious. The apartment they had rented on via Albalonga was too small. The city was full of the noise of endless modernization ordered by Mussolini. She no longer recognized the streets and sights of her youth. Many had been razed to make way for the EUR, Mussolini's concept of a modern Rome. Then there was the frightening omnipresence of Blackshirts. Maddalena begged to return home. Ida finally gave in.

Federico reflected on his mother's departure. He had lost no time finding an apartment closer to the center of Rome. It was a tiny room with a dingy shared bathroom down the hall. The room was situated in a larger house that had a variety of other renters. On his initial visit there was an old actor, a university professor, and the constant chatter of the children of the owner. The owner herself was a large woman, bedridden, who had ordered Federico into her boudoir for a once-over. Evidently he had passed her test. The room was his. He could come and go when he pleased. All of Rome was just outside his door. He could savor it anytime he chose.

He had to answer to no one except his new employer, the editor at *Marc'Aurelio*. As a teenager in Rimini, Federico had read the satirical magazine, one of the most popular in Italy, particularly among young people. He had submitted to the magazine and met one of its editors by chance on the beach in Rimini. The editor had told Federico to "look him up," a casual invitation Federico had pursued with fanatical determination once he arrived in Rome.

After some false starts and rejections, De Bolles, the editor, had finally accepted one of Federico's illustrations. This led to some assignments for articles. Federico's work began to be noticed by other editors and colleagues at the magazine. He had quickly become known for his wit, his ability to produce collaboratively and with a distinctive flair.

Federico gazed with appreciation at his first paycheck. It meant freedom. It meant that he had talent, recognizable talent, for which people were willing to pay. He stretched out his long legs and surveyed his torn canvas shoes. Perhaps a portion of the paycheck could remedy that. He ran his hands through his long, tangled hair. It stood on end like a haystack. He chuckled to himself. He had freedom from his family, a room of his own, a paycheck in his pocket. Rome was laid out at his feet. Life was good.

Suddenly he was punched from behind. He turned and found two Blackshirts staring at him.

"Get up. Get going. Bums should move along."

Federico did not argue. The square was filling up anyway and his celebratory mood was waning as the exhaustion of having stayed up all night began to settle. De Bolles and the other editors at *Marc'Aurelio* were waiting. They didn't care if he had stayed up all night. There was an issue to get out. As he made his way to his new apartment, newspaper boys hawked the headlines; they were all about the Italian invasion of Albania.

With an espresso for fortification, Federico entered the

offices of *Marc'Aurelio* an hour later. The magazine shared the building with other printed publications, such as the newspaper *Il Piccolino.* The hallways and offices were perpetually packed with people. No one ever seemed to sit at a desk. There was a constant buzzing cacophony. There were shelves filled with drawings and prototypes, illustrations for upcoming issues leaned against walls, stacks of printed paper, copies of previous issues, empty food cartons, and overflowing ashtrays. Cartoonists, illustrators, journalists, photographers, novelists, playwrights, artists, opinion writers, and advertisers filled the offices, gesticulating, sitting atop desks, stretching out with their feet splayed into the narrow passages between desks. The chief editor was arguing about the wisdom of printing an illustration that insinuated one of Mussolini's ministers was a glutton. Another columnist vociferously defended his friend's position. Others in the room joined in. The noise in the rooms rose, at times, to a decibel that drove the writers to the small caffès that lined the street below to get actual work done.

One of the other young writers at *Marc'Aurelio* was Ruggero Maccari, whose dream was to write for films. He went to see them every night and often took Federico along. Federico was still enamored of the idea of being a journalist. He got it from the American film *The Front Page.* He imagined himself a hardboiled reporter with a trench coat and a porkpie hat perched on the back of his head.

He did one assignment as a straight reporter: He interviewed all of the people involved in a murder investigation. The resulting article was a story he fabricated, weak on facts but vastly entertaining. His talent was undeniable and the wise editors saw a way to put it to excellent use. He was quickly assigned to write weekly advice columns that combined humor and a perspective on a wide variety of life situations. One of his first was a column titled "Will You Listen to What I Have to Say?" It dispensed advice on love and life from the perspective of a wide variety of characters. It gave Federico a chance to write in the voices of a dizzying array of professions, genders, and walks of life.

The editorial meetings at *Il Popolo di Roma,* another newspaper for which Federico wrote, went on for hours. All the Roman newspapers had to tread the razor-thin line between stating the facts and keeping within the boundaries of Fascist censorship. There was plenty to discuss at editorial meetings.

On September 1, 1939, Hitler invaded Poland and World War II began. With Italy and Germany allied, Italian participation in the coming war was inevitable. Fascist censorship grew more stringent.

When Federico wrote a column in the voice of a young girl frightened during an air raid, the entire staff at *Il Popolo* was called into the Fascist headquarters. A stiff, humorless lieutenant walked down the line of employees asking them what they did at the newspaper.

When Federico was questioned, he answered honestly, "Will You Listen to What I Have to Say?"

The soldier did a double take and answered, "Well, yes, of course." He took a moment to size up Federico. "I would strongly suggest you cut your hair."

The journalists were dismissed. But the experience began to sour Federico on working at newspapers.

He continued to work as a columnist, illustrator, and freelance writer for various publications, including a cinema magazine for which he did interviews. When the cacophony of the *Marc'Aurelio* offices grew too loud even for Federico, he would escape to via Veneto, the street that ran alongside the *Marc'Aurelio* offices. Its wide avenue, lined by chestnut trees, climbed up a sloping hill, curving from the Piazza Barberini. It was dotted with caffès and bars with striped awnings to shade patrons from the afternoon sun.

Federico began his strolls there, often with his new friend Rinaldo Geleng, a young painter who had moved to Rome a year before Federico. Geleng knew all the restaurants that would serve starving artists with food left over at the end of the night. Cesarina became one of their favorites. Federico never forgot their generosity to young artists.

The two young men walked the streets of Rome for hours, never tiring of the human entertainment; they found fascination in the street walkers and their customers, the street sweepers, the caffè owners, the beggars, the nightlife that populated every square, the *carabinieri* (policemen), and even the omnipresent Blackshirts who patrolled Rome in ever-increasing numbers.

Federico and Geleng also roamed the restaurants, making money by offering to do portraits of patrons. Geleng was better at capturing exact likenesses. Federico's portraits inevitably seemed to include his opinion of the subject: eyes became glaring and enlarged, hairdos exaggerated, the inner souls of the subjects exposed through Federico's unique vision. One husband, whose portly wife became decidedly porcine under Federico's gaze, became enraged. Others were enchanted by Federico's artistry. Geleng recommended Federico to a window designer, giving him oil paints that ran down the window in rivulets, leaving the shop owner apoplectic.

Federico, Geleng, Ruggero Maccari, and other young artists did not have much money, but they had enough to get by. They were living in a city that was on the brink of war. The Fascist regime kept every artist on edge. They teetered between repression and expression. And yet, Federico was happy. He was free to pursue his artistic interests. He wandered the streets of Rome at night, hungry but full of excitement and curiosity. The melancholy piazzas and squares with the late-night sounds of splashing fountains and whistling wind embraced him, caressed him, sustained him. Rome became his mother.

One of Federico's assignments came from the magazine *Cinemamaggazino,* a publication that featured interviews with celebrities as well as up-and-coming film actors and directors. Federico was given an interview with the actor Osvaldo Valenti, who was starring in *La Corona di Ferro,* a film directed by Alessandro Blasetti. Valenti had come up through the ubiquitous "white telephone" comedies of Italian cinema in the late thirties. Featuring comic situations and women in peignoirs with fluffy slippers and white telephones, these light entertainments had bourgeoisie appeal that made Valenti a favorite. The sword-and-sandal epics found favor with audiences as well. They were also given the seal of approval from the Fascist censors, who approved any entertainment that included war scenes trumpeting Italian military might.

For his interview with Valenti, Federico made his first visit to one of the crown jewels of Mussolini's reconstruction of Roman life and culture: the film studio Cinecittà. Literally meaning "City of Cinema," Cinecittà had opened on April 21, 1937. Founded by Mussolini, the motto of the studio was "Cinema is the most powerful weapon." The opening day was chosen strategically as it was supposedly the day of the founding of Rome itself. Mussolini brought all of his military pomp to celebrate the day, which marked a milestone in the Fascist regime. Supported by Mussolini but administered by his son Vittorio, a noted cinephile, Cinecittà represented the ultimate in modern achievement. It was the largest and most advanced film studio in Europe. Built outside of Rome on one hundred and thirty acres, the studio boasted nineteen soundstages that contained the latest in technological capabilities. Cinecittà boasted four restaurants and a manmade lake. It was interspersed with manicured gardens, splashing fountains, and intricately landscaped pathways. Visitors to the studio were greeted by massive statuary and crisply uniformed guards.

It was early June, 1940, and twenty-year-old Federico made his way to the three-year-old studio about which he had heard so much. The guards sneered at him as they took in his wrinkled linen shirt and scuffed shoes. Federico could not have cared less; he was fascinated by finally getting through the gates of the famed studio. The heel of his canvas shoe eventually gave way and he had no choice but to hobble along, marveling at the bushes clipped into the shapes of mythological creatures. He was given a map of the studio and directed to Osvaldo Valenti's dressing room.

Federico was in awe. To his left was a massive lake. Three ships dressed to look like seventeenth-century pirate brigantines floated on the water. To his right were three soundstages with the doors wide open. Men and women rushed about in a beehive of activity. He passed a restaurant filled with actors who sat at long tables. They were dressed in every kind of costume imaginable: priests, butchers, kings, queens, chefs with toque hats, opera divas, men sporting top hats. One man was wearing the bottom half of a zebra suit. There were young women dressed as ballerinas and nightclub dancers. Some wore the barest of swimsuits with white terrycloth robes draped casually over their shoulders. They were all eating lunch, drinking wine, and sipping coffee. A bell rang, presumably calling them back to their respective sets, and they dispersed amid hugs, laughter, and promises to meet later for drinks.

Federico wondered if he had gone to heaven. It was the friendliest, most congenial gathering he had ever witnessed.

He walked, dazed, down a dirt pathway. He followed three shapely actresses who were dressed in togas. As he pondered what miracle of costuming held up the flimsy material, he heard shouting but couldn't place its origin. The three girls stopped, giggled, and pointed upward. Federico shaded his eyes, scanning the blue June sky above Cinecittà. He followed the arm of what appeared to be a crane. At the end of the crane was a bucket. On top of the bucket was a platform with a railing. Perched atop the platform was a man dressed in leather puttees. He was wielding a bullhorn, waving at someone, and shouting, "Get out of my shot! Get the hell out of my shot!" The girls began roaring with laughter.

Federico realized it was the director and that he was the object of the man's ire. He was not walking on a pathway, but a road in ancient Thebes. The girls in front of him were not casually walking; they were acting in a scene.

As he scurried away, he caught sight of a crowd of extras. There must have been at least two hundred of them. Some were frozen in place. Others were conversing, finishing cigarettes, and stamping out butts as they heard the word "Rolling!" When the director yelled "Action!" they began screaming and writhing in agony; their eyes filled with fear and loathing and some fell to the ground in abject terror. When the director yelled "Cut!" they went immediately back to their flirtations and smokes, as if nothing had happened. It was all a part of a day's work at Cinecittà. To Federico, it was absolute magic. He was entranced. He could hardly believe a universe existed in which hundreds of people did exactly what one wanted at the sound of one word: "Action!"

Federico finally found his way to Valenti's dressing room. The actor lounged on a velvet settee, languidly smoking, and couldn't be bothered to rise from his supine position. He barely acknowledged Federico. Two young women fluttered around him. One arranged pastries on a tray. The other massaged his shoulders.

"This is a back-breaking role and I need all the assistance I can get," he said.

Federico was dumbfounded. "Is this how everyone on the film is treated?" he blurted out. As the words came out of his mouth, he knew it was the wrong thing to say.

Valenti lurched up as if he had been stung by a bee. "Most certainly not. Only the stars." He regarded Federico with contempt. "Those who revere and love Il Duce are respected the most." He gestured to a large portrait of Mussolini that occupied an entire wall of the room.

Federico found Valenti to be deeply narcissistic. The interview did not go well. But it had brought him to Cinecittà. To think that all of this was going on just three miles from the center of Rome. It was a world where dreams were made real.

Federico continued to make money writing advice columns. Although he was only twenty, the columns gave him license to contemplate and reveal his thoughts on living in an urban environment like Rome, tasting its pleasures and overcoming its challenges. One particularly poignant column was full of advice on how to spend a birthday alone. Federico was experiencing both the joys and the occasional melancholy of life as a young writer in Rome at the beginning of a new decade.

On July 10, 1940, Federico strolled down via Veneto on his way to the *Marc'Aurelio* offices. He found the streets strangely empty. He couldn't afford to eat in any of the caffès on the street, but he often stopped for a morning espresso. He needed one this morning as he had been out late at his favorite restaurant,

Cesarina, with the garrulous editor Garrone, who had generously treated him. The table was full of journalists and writers, including Ennio Flaiano, a deeply intellectual man who had begun his career as a lawyer, but decided to move his family to Rome and start a new life as a playwright and screenwriter. The conversation at the table revolved around politics and the coming war. The subjects bored Federico.

Garrone was smart, experienced, and generous, and loved telling tales. His favorite pastime was sharing meals and wisdom with younger writers. He called Federico "The Kid" and was a sort of father figure to him. Federico rarely heard from his own father and felt he was a disappointment to him. Urbano had visited Rome once, arranging a brief luncheon with his son and leaving abruptly, Federico was sure, for an assignation—the true reason for his visit to Rome. Federico loved and appreciated Garrone. But he also realized the editor represented the sort of man he didn't want to become: a person reduced to resting on his laurels and boring young people with tales of his misspent youth.

Federico continued his walk toward the *Marc'Aurelio* offices. The chestnut trees on via Veneto shimmered in the June breeze. Not a soul appeared on the street.

He walked into a small coffee bar, his favorite. Mario, the owner, greeted him with a distracted wave. Then Federico heard the rasping voice of Il Duce blaring out of the radio. Mario was glued to the radio and made no move to serve Federico. The first words Federico heard were "the declaration of war has already been handed over to the ambassadors." The speech was interrupted by the deafening cheers of thousands. The speech went on ". . . of Great Britain and France. We take to the field against the plutocratic and reactionary democracies of the west. Italy proletarian and Fascist takes to the field . . . it already shifts and lights the hearts from the Apennines to the Indian Ocean: We will win!" There was more deafening cheering. Mussolini stopped speaking to revel in the sound. "Run to arms and show your tenacity, your courage, your value."

Mario snapped off the radio. He limped to the espresso machine and poured out a steaming cup. He served it with a slice of lemon that he deftly cut, wiping the knife blade on his apron.

"Hello Fefe," he said. He knew Federico well by this time and called him by his nickname. He pointed to his leg and said, "Crushed by a German feldkanone in the Battle of the Somme. I wanted to be a writer, too, but you see, my mind was gone after that. Couldn't think straight."

He leaned close to Federico and grabbed him by the ragged shirt collar. "You've got two jobs now, Fefe. Writing. And staying out of this damned war." His eyes were wide with fear. He let go of Federico, saying, "I like you, Fefe. Don't end up like me."

Federico gulped his espresso. It was hot and it burned his throat. He suddenly felt as if he were suffocating. He walked outside and began to cross via Veneto. He was nearly run over by an adolescent boy on a bicycle. The boy was gliding down the street with his legs akimbo. He threw his cap in the air, exposing his cherubic cheeks.

"Yay . . . war has been declared!" the boy yelled.

Mario limped up behind Federico. "Within three years he'll be lying in pieces in a foxhole. Guaranteed. Don't forget what I said."

Federico took the warning seriously. In addition to his work as a journalist and illustrator, dodging the armed services became a part-time job. He had experienced heart murmurs since he was a child and at first he got letters of medical deferment from doctors recommended by Garrone.

His interest in journalism began to wane, partly because of two friendships he made. Sent to interview the up-and-coming actor Aldo Fabrizi, Federico was reintroduced to a world that had always appealed to him. The article was a comical take on the view from an actor's dressing room.

The young journalist and the actor, who was fifteen years older than Federico, took an immediate liking to one another. They met backstage in Fabrizi's dressing room at the Jovinelli Theater. Dating from 1906, the Jovinelli was a comedy and variety theater built for just such entertainment. Comedians, clowns, and lowbrow singers appealed to crowds who needed a respite from the daily grind and the war.

It was just the sort of place that appealed to Federico. He was not as enamored of the deep, intellectual conversations that took place among his fellow journalists during endless dinners at Cesarina and around the desks at *Marc'Aurelio.* The camaraderie of the actors and the skill of their performances charmed and tantalized Federico. He felt at home there. Highbrow intellectuals like the writer Ennio Flaiano, with years of higher education and degrees, were a part of Federico's life, but they were not his favorites. He was attracted to the performers with a background in vaudeville, who entertained the working class with comedy, slapstick, drag, dancing, and singing at variety halls that proliferated around Rome.

The first time Federico met Fabrizi, he found the actor at a rickety dressing table fifteen minutes before showtime. Federico sat with a pencil poised over his writing pad. Fabrizi's large, well-shaped hand clamped down and covered the pad.

"You don't need to write down a thing," Fabrizi said. "Believe me. I'm not going to say anything profound. Write about the whole thing—the poverty, the voices, the wish to communicate the miracle of art for the people, not for those snobs on via Veneto. Go out and see the show. We'll talk after. Better yet, we'll eat after. You look like you could use a bite or two."

With that, Fabrizi returned to his mirror. In a few quick swipes, his olive complexion became white. He jumped into a pair of baggy striped pants with wide suspenders.

"There is no dignity here," he continued. "Not the kind you usually think of . . . but there is dignity in what we do. No high art. The people don't need high art right now. They need a laugh. Stand backstage before the show and look out. You'll see what I mean."

Federico did just that on his way from backstage to the audience. He peeked at the crowd through the battered velvet curtain. There were people of all ages. There were small children who climbed from seat to seat. There were young girls who leaned over the rail to the orchestra pit, flirting with the musicians. There were candy sellers hawking Jordan almonds and *bomboniere.* One toddler began to relieve himself in the aisle. He was swept up by his mother and scolded by an elderly patron. A haze of cigarette smoke hung in the air and the cacophony of voices rose to crescendo as the lights began to go down. The audience began clapping in anticipation as the orchestra struck up "Ultime Foglie," a popular tune. The crowd began to sing along. Federico took his seat, squeezing between a group of sailors and a family with three children who bounced on their parents' laps in time to the music. He sang at the top of his lungs along with the rest of the rowdy audience.

Federico and Fabrizi adjourned to the Caffè Castellino after the show, which let out at midnight. Fabrizi told Federico about his life as a young actor in Rome and the joys and tribulations of a life on the road in a traveling acting company. By the time their meal was finished, it was three o'clock in the morning. The two men walked home toward Fabrizi's apartment at via Sannio 37. They sat on the marble steps of the Scala Santa. The holy staircase was situated at the east side of Piazza di San Giovanni.

"It has twenty-eight steps," said Fabrizi. "Jesus himself was said to have walked these steps. They were once in Pilate's house. They are holy. Are you religious, Fefe?" Fabrizi was already comfortable enough to call Federico by his pet name. "These are the steps on which Pilate condemned Jesus. Think of it. This is the people's sanctuary. The gates are usually locked up tight at this part of the night. But tonight, they were wide open. You must have magic powers, my friend."

The two friends sat in the velvety darkness of the Roman

night. They looked out and saw stars hanging over the Porta Asinaria.

Fabrizi pointed to where they were looking. "You know what they call that, right? The Gate of the Donkeys. And here we are. Hee-haw," he laughed.

The stars twinkled over the ancient gates. They could hear the clang of chairs being brought into the caffès that would soon open again to serve rich espresso, *cornetti* pastries, and *fette biscottate* cookies to early morning patrons. Someone laughed in a distant alley; it was a flirtatious, tinkling sound.

"Rome embraces you, doesn't it?" said Federico. "It is a sort of religion within a religion."

"You've got a way with words, Fefe," said Fabrizi admiringly. "Have you ever thought of writing for the stage? Or better yet, for radio? They are aching for content. Hell, I am aching for content. I'll hire you!"

Aldo Fabrizi was as good as his word. He hired Federico to write monologues for him. As other performers saw the way audiences responded to the material, they hired Federico as well. He was introduced to many actors, among them Alberto Sordi, a round-faced comedian who performed at variety theaters, worked in film, and also dubbed Italian versions of Laurel and Hardy. Like Fabrizi, Sordi worked in *avanspettacolo,* live entertainments that were interludes between films—a holdover from the silent film era and vaudeville days. In the dairy shop they frequented on via Frattina, Sordi, too, encouraged Federico to begin writing dialogue.

Federico did not need much encouragement. Used to working collaboratively and quickly, he began writing radio scripts. Teaming with Ruggero Maccari, Federico wrote "The Match," about the struggles of a love relationship. It aired on December 12, 1940—his first radio script to air. Fabrizi also introduced Federico to writers in the film community. It wasn't long before Federico began to contribute to screenplays, giving suggestions, coming up with storylines and ideas, and providing dialogue. Writer Cesare Zavattini and director Alberto Lattuada were colleagues with whom Federico began to collaborate. Almost immediately the gritty, realistic takes these men had on script and character were different from those of elitists like Vittorio De Sica, whose style was elegant and removed from the everyday lives of modern Italians. This schism between what some felt was the "anti-intellectualism" of artists like Fellini and the cultured elitism of De Sica would last for decades.

On August 30, 1942, *Before the Postman* became Federico's first film credit. Sitting in the theater and watching his name appear on the screen in the murky darkness of the theater was a thrill that took him back to his first night at the Fulgor. The film was a modest success at the box office, but it cemented his collaborative relationship with Aldo Fabrizi and stood as his professional entry into the world of film.

He continued to work both in the medium of radio and film, providing scripts for radio shows and acting as an advisor to colleagues who were writing screenplays. His circle of friendships had moved away from journalists and magazine writers to the world of actors, screenwriters, and directors.

As the war raged in Europe and conscriptions became more prevalent, Federico, along with all young men of age to serve, had to either join the army or provide medical proof that they were physically incapable of serving. Federico's services as a script collaborator were in demand. He was thrilled to be asked by Vittorio Mussolini to collaborate on the script for *Knights of the Desert,* an adventure film being shot in Libya. Based on a novel by Emilio Salgari, it was being co-directed by Gino Talamo and Osvaldo Valenti. As shooting was about to begin, Federico was asked by production to go on location. The request would allow him to go to a part of the world he had never seen. It would also take him out of Rome and away from the draft board.

Federico eagerly climbed aboard a rickety two-seater provided by the production company and found himself outside Tripoli with an underfunded production, weak directors who fought constantly, and a discouraged, demoralized cast and crew. When Talamo became disabled in a car accident, Federico was asked to take over shooting for a day. The conditions could not have been worse. The heat was relentless and the actors were listless and angry.

The shooting schedule for the day included a love scene. It was up first thing and Federico was in charge. It had all happened so quickly. On the morning of November 14, 1942, Federico stepped behind the camera for the first time and took in the sight of the two leads. They were framed in a two shot. They were staring listlessly at one another. Federico's heart was pounding so hard he was afraid he would shake the camera. Just as suddenly, a sense of calm came over him. He knew immediately that the scene was about the woman—it needed to be shot from her point of view. He began directing the crew to move the camera and started a conversation with the actress; they were talking about her character, something she had never considered before. She seemed shocked that the director was actually talking to her. She was just beginning to come alive, to respond to Federico. Everything else fell away and Federico was completely involved in the moment.

Later that same day, American forces began engaging with German forces in the Battle of El Alamein. It was clear that their location would quickly become a battlefield. German aircraft carriers picked up the terrified cast and crew to fly them back to Rome. As they made their way up the coast of Italy, they were targeted by Allied firepower. Federico never forgot the sound of flak hitting the side of the plane. Deeply shaken, he returned to Rome grateful to have survived. Still, despite the disarray of the shoot, he couldn't forget the feeling of anticipation and excitement that had filled his mind when he took over as director, even for a few hours. He wanted to have that again.

On his return to Rome, Federico immediately went back to work writing radio scripts and contributing to screenplays. A new radio series was about to begin and Federico was tasked with casting the actors. He began what would become a lifelong habit of going through stacks of photographs and possibilities. The new show was titled *Chico and Paulina*. It detailed, in a comic fashion, the domestic ups and downs of a young romantic couple. Federico went through stacks of hopefuls; jobs were getting harder and harder to come by and the response to the casting call had been massive. There were glamorous women with swooping curvy bangs in the fashion of American actress Veronica Lake. There were hundreds of full-body shots of actresses with hourglass figures and seductively draped clothing. Some wore hardly any clothing at all.

And then Federico was stopped by the photograph of a face that seemed to float off the page. It was a face like no other. It was utterly different from anyone else. Her hair was dark and curly and framed her heart-shaped face. She had pale, translucent skin and no trace of makeup. Her dark, round eyes stared out of the photo in a manner that seemed to convey both supreme confidence and infinite vulnerability. Federico held the photograph in his hands as if it were a sacred thing.

"She is as mysterious as the Mona Lisa," said Federico to Maccari. "I have found my Paulina."

"You haven't even heard her speak. How do you know how she sounds?"

"I have a hunch. I'll call her right now," said Federico, dialing the number on the back of the photograph.

"You and your hunches," laughed Maccari.

A woman with a low, mellifluous voice answered.

"I am looking for Giulia Masina," Federico said. He put his hand over the phone, addressing Maccari: "Her voice is beautiful."

"I'm her aunt," said the voice. "What is this about?"

Federico turned to Maccari with a frown.

He explained to the woman that he was a writer working on casting for a radio show. There was a long pause, as if the woman were deciding how legitimate this sounded.

"I'll get her."

Apparently he had passed some sort of test. Federico waited, literally crossing his fingers, while Maccari pelted him with spitballs.

"I am Giulia," said a voice so low it was barely discernible. It was like velvet mixed with bittersweet chocolate.

Federico leapt up with happiness. The phone nearly disconnected from the wall. By the end of the conversation, they had made a lunch date. Federico had considered a dinner date, but felt lunch would be more professional. They arranged to meet the next day in the Piazza Barberini near the Triton Fountain.

Federico's heart pounded as he pawed through a pile of wrinkled shirts and chose the least threadbare. His white canvas shoes had faded to yellow. In lieu of an iron, which he didn't own, he placed his chosen shirt and pants between his mattress and the springs and lay on his bed. He turned on his stomach and grabbed for the paper and pencils he always kept nearby. He felt like sketching. It quickly became the smiling face of a young woman with intelligent dark eyes.

For her part, Giulia Masina prepared carefully in her aunt's via Lutezia apartment. Her family had allowed her to go to live with her aunt in Rome on the agreement that she would follow the highest standards of ethics and behavior. Her aunt Giulia Pasqualina supported her niece in all of her artistic aspirations.

There had never been a problem as Giulia was one of the most highly disciplined people her aunt had ever known.

She had eaten lunch with her aunt, not wanting to tell her that she was meeting a scriptwriter for the radio. It was hard to find makeup in the stores as rationing limited supplies. Giulia used a burnt match stick to darken her eyebrows. She had a tiny bit of lipstick left and used it for rouge and a touch on her lips.

Giulia stared at herself in the mirror. She could see the child who had grown up in San Giorgio di Piano in an artistic family. Her father was a violinist. Her mother was a teacher. They had artistic friends and acquaintances. Giulia remembered meeting the playwright Luigi Pirandello when she was a child. Her uncle in Rome had taken a special interest in her and encouraged her to study singing and dancing as a young child. When he passed away, his wife in Rome suggested the family might allow their teenage daughter to move to Rome to take advantage of the cultural life and instructors there.

Even as an adolescent, Giulia began to demonstrate extraordinary talents in movement and mimicry. She was focused and took her studies seriously. Although her parents wanted her to become a dancer, her diminutive size precluded that career. As a grown woman, she was barely five feet tall. Her stage presence, however, was undeniable and they allowed her to move to Rome with their blessing. Initially she attended an Ursuline convent in Rome and studied voice, piano, and dance.

Ultimately she attended the Sapienza University of Rome and majored in literature. But her real love was the Gruppo

Universitari Fascisti at the university, an experimental group set up under the aegis of the Fascist party to promote culture among young people. It was a part of Mussolini's plan for a "new Italy." The troupe was a chance for Giulia to display her dazzling talent. On one triple bill, she played a middle-aged mother in Thornton Wilder's *The Happy Journey to Trenton and Camden,* a fourteen-year-old boy in Rabindranath Tagore's *The Post Office,* and a prostitute in Pirandello's *The Way Out.* Her work in theater was praised for its complexity and variety. Although her family insisted she complete her university degree, her career path was clear: Giulia was going to be an actress.

In 1942, she jumped at the chance to work in radio. Simply put, it paid better than the theater. It was something she could do while finishing her degree. Film work, on the other hand, was a mystery to her. She did not look anything like the curvaceous beauties who populated the screens in the current batch of white telephone films. Weighing ninety-three pounds and with a gamine appearance, Giulia was confident in her throaty voice and ability to work in radio.

It was a sunny day in early February, but there was a sharp wind blowing in the Piazza Barberini. As Federico rounded the corner into the wide plaza, he saw the Triton Fountain. The wind was blowing the water that splashed from Triton's mouth. Directly underneath it stood a tiny woman in a purple plaid coat. She wore a matching wool beret. With Triton in the background, she looked as though she could be a sea nymph. As Federico walked toward her, she waved excitedly. Her mouth broke into a smile as wide as the Tiber. Federico towered over her. She was so tiny he wanted to lift her in his arms. She looked up at him with eyes that seemed to hold the wisdom of the ages. The rest of the world seemed to fall away. Nothing else existed. He could have been staring at her for a second or for hours. Time no longer had any meaning.

A roaring scooter shot around the fountain. It carried a Blackshirt and nearly knocked them over. He sped off and looked back at them as though they had been at fault. Giulia jumped to the side and grabbed Federico's arm. He placed his large hand over her tiny one and they walked, holding one another, to the nearby restaurant. It seemed as natural as the midday sun that warmed them. The red geraniums in the window boxes of the restaurant were just beginning to bloom. It was a fancy eatery, with white linen tablecloths and attentive waiters.

"You are the perfect Paulina," Federico began. "I knew it the minute I heard your voice. Aldo Fabrizi told me about your performances at the university. I'm not highbrow enough to attend such things," Federico put his hand on his heart with a modest bow of his head. "I've been too focused on gags and vaudeville to attend these intellectual enterprises. You must forgive me."

Giulia laughed. "I'm flattered, Federico, but I would hardly call you a gag writer." She smiled at him. Her eyes twinkled.

"Call me Fefe. All my friends do."

Federico ordered *crostini bianchi* (ricotta and anchovy canapes), roasted peppers, anchovies, and *gamberetti all'olio e limone*—the poached shrimp dish was a favorite of his grandmother in Gambettola. These were just the appetizers. He then ordered risotto and two main dishes, including *abbachio,* a roast lamb with rosemary.

Giulia's eyes grew even larger. She looked around the restaurant. The waiters fluttered about. She wondered how this young man with the torn canvas shoes, tattered shirt, and unruly hair could afford such a meal. She reached out for his hands and took them into her small ones.

"Soup is good enough for me," she said.

"Miss Giulia . . ." he began.

"You can call me Giulietta," she smiled. "All my good friends do."

"You must understand," he answered, "this is my celebration. I have found my Paulina. And my Giulietta."

They stayed at the restaurant until the late afternoon sun began to cast shadows on the terra cotta floor tiles. The waiters began sweeping up, readying the dining room for the dinner crowd; they had scraped all the crumbs from their tablecloth. The bill was presented and Federico pulled out a huge roll of money. Giulietta couldn't help but stare.

"Just in case you thought I was some kind of bum," said Federico, "you see there is money to be made in radio!"

He tipped the waiters generously and they obligingly brought a final aperitif: amaretto liqueur.

Federico walked Giulietta home along the Tiber. Evening was beginning to descend. The February wind blew off the river. Giulietta shivered and Federico put his arm around her. Giulietta leaned her head against his arm. They were already so comfortable with one another they didn't need to speak. As they arrived at via Lutezia 14, Giulietta's aunt's apartment, Federico looked into Giulietta's eyes. He began to say "Can I see you tomorrow?" but he was unable to finish his request. She had already said "Yes."

From their first meeting, Federico and Giulietta were rarely seen apart. His friends Rinaldo Geleng, Aldo Fabrizi, and Alberto Sordi grew used to seeing them together, locked in intimate conversation. *Chico and Paulina* proved to be an audience favorite. It aired every Sunday evening. Listeners seemed delighted to delve into the world of romance and domesticity; they were eager to escape, for a few moments, the increasingly desperate situation in the outer world. Allied forces, it was rumored, were preparing to land in Sicily. Strategic bombing had already begun up and down the coast of Italy.

In the midst of the continuing crisis, Federico and Giulietta found a haven in each other. They worked together as writer and actress on *Chico and Paulina*. Federico found, in Giulietta and in her aunt, acceptance and encouragement. Wherever his wanderings around Rome took him, whatever challenge his creative life brought to him now, there was a warm, welcoming place for him. He began spending more and more time at the apartment on via Lutezia. In Federico, Giulietta discovered a fellow artist who appreciated the width and breadth of her talent, who found her capability infinite and who was inspired by her commitment to her work. If the city of Rome was his mother, Giulietta became his heart. She was more wonderful than anything he could have dreamed.

The real world soon intruded. Federico received a draft

notice that was signed by a German officer. He reported to the recruitment office in Bologna on May 16, 1943. This time, there would be no getting out with a doctor's letter. Nevertheless, Federico ran up and down nearby stairs for half an hour prior to the examination in order to get his heart racing. Nazi officers were indeed overseeing the proceedings and they deemed him physically sound. The doctor left the exam room after having presented Federico with an officially stamped order to present himself for service.

Federico was putting on his shoes when an air raid siren sounded. There was a loud, ear-splitting whistle. Then a bomb landed directly on the hospital. The floor on which Federico stood collapsed. Miraculously, Federico landed on his feet on the first floor. Shattered glass and rubble began pouring through the hole. The sounds of screams and the collapsing structure followed him as he picked his way through a shattered window.

He ran for his life, not knowing whether to expect another bomb or a Nazi bullet in his back. A produce truck going toward Rome picked him up. He was dropped off in the outskirts; he could see the Dome of St. Peter's rising in the distance, welcoming him, just as he had as a young boy the first time he had come to Rome. The order to report for duty was in his pocket. He took it out, tore it up, and threw the pieces in the Tiber. He was free again—for the moment. War seemed to remove all expectation of certainty. But Federico was sure of one thing: No matter what else happened, he was going to marry Giulietta Masina.

The war became an omnipresent monster sucking the life

out of the city and its citizens. On returning to Rome, Federico found that the rumor that a thousand Jews had been rounded up and deported from the ancient Portico d'Ottavia section of the city, the heart of the Jewish ghetto, was true. A truck filled with four hundred SS soldiers had pulled up and fanned out in the quarter, which occupied a four-block area near the Tiber. Within a few hours, they had gone door to door arresting anyone they found and deported them to labor camps. Some said they were not labor camps, but death camps. Federico had loved walking there to taste the delicacies from its bake shops. They were all closed now. An eerie silence filled the once-bustling square.

When the Allies landed in Sicily on July 10, 1943, the war became ever present. Bombings increased in cities along the coast. The Allies were softening Italy up for the ground invasion. Federico and Giulietta heard from their families sporadically. Urbano, Ida, and Maddalena left Rimini to seek refuge in San Marino. Rimini was ultimately bombed 397 times. Giulietta told her parents of her engagement, but there was no possibility of planning a wedding. Finally, communication outside Rome was cut off.

On the night of July 16, 1943, Allied bombs hit Rome's San Lorenzo district, a working-class neighborhood near a factory. The bombing killed 166 civilians and severely damaged the ancient chapel San Lorenzo fuori le Mura. On August 13, Mussolini was deposed and Marshal Badoglio was installed. He pledged allegiance to the Axis powers, but fearing his weakness, the Germans decided to take over the city.

On September 11, 1943, partisans, police, and even citizens

as young as fourteen fought to prevent the Germans from entering Rome. They were slaughtered. The Germans occupied Rome the next day. They called Rome an "open city." It was a cruel misnomer. They set up headquarters on via Tasso. Anyone arrested and sent there could be assured of interrogation, torture, and, in most cases, death by slow degrees. Federico joined nearly two hundred thousand young men who hid out in the apartments, basements, and alleyways of Rome, hoping to evade conscription, capture, or torture.

It was an inauspicious time for a marriage. But on October 30, 1943, Federico and Giulietta were married by a neighboring priest. The ceremony was held in her aunt's apartment. Federico made the invitations that depicted the lovers floating on clouds, connected by a *bambino.* They celebrated the day, sneaking out to a theater where Alberto Sordi was performing. When he saw his newly married friend, Sordi had a spotlight directed to the young couple. He introduced them, saying, "I couldn't be at their wedding, I can't afford a present, but I want to give the gift of applause. The first in a long career."

The audience craned their necks to see the young groom with a shock of dark hair. He had his arm around the shoulders of an angelic-looking young woman who had a smile as wide as the Tiber. The couple stood and bowed graciously. Inside the theater, the temple of art and joy, they clung to one another. The audience applauded. Then an air raid siren sounded. Everyone hit the floor.

Chapter Four

THE DREAM OF REALITY

Was it too much to ask, even during the German occupation, to get one's new bride some coffee on her first morning as a married woman? Federico didn't think so. Auntie Giulia had gone to the neighbor's apartment the night before to give them privacy for their honeymoon evening. The dear woman had scrounged sugar from somewhere and made them a tiny wedding cake. Giulietta had begged Federico to not go out for coffee or anything else. It was too dangerous. There were daily roundups. It was rumored that thousands of young men just like Federico were in hiding all over Rome. Giulietta, Federico, and Auntie had devised a plan to push an ancient wardrobe in front of a tiny closet where Federico would hide should the SS arrive at their door. All apartment buildings, office buildings, parks, and public places were subject to constant raids.

Federico glanced at his new wife, blissfully asleep on the tiny bed. It fit her, he thought. His long legs dangled off the end. It was not a bed made for a tall man. He crept out the door and down to via Lutezia. He had heard there was a black-market seller of real coffee just off Piazza di Spagna—if you got there early. He hadn't been out in daylight in weeks. He had been submitting rewrites and ideas for screenplays and radio plays through Giulietta; she transported his work back and forth and they managed to cobble together some money. But as the German occupation dragged on, work had begun to dry up.

Federico made his way around the Villa Borghese gardens. It was oddly warm for the first day of November. He was a newly married man. He would never be lonely again. Federico took a deep breath. He felt a tiny release of the tension that seemed to envelop the whole city on a daily basis. It was like wearing a thick overcoat that one could never remove.

As he approached the Piazza di Spagna, he saw three women standing in a circle. He had seen hardly any other people on his walk. They looked out of place standing together like that. They beckoned to him. Federico couldn't imagine what they wanted. He felt slightly uneasy but it wasn't polite to ignore women in possible distress. As he neared the group, he felt something hard and round at his back. The women ran up the Spanish Steps and disappeared.

Federico realized too late it had been a trap. He heard the sound of a truck grinding into gear. It pulled up in front of him. As Federico peered into it, he saw the grimy faces of men of all ages. There were boys barely old enough for puberty and old men with white in their beards. Nazi soldiers with machine guns jumped off the sides of the truck and said one word to Federico: "Schnell" ("Quickly"). They looked nearly as exhausted as the conscripts. They were not in a mood to forgive hesitation.

Federico climbed into the truck. One man began to speak. He was batted into unconsciousness with the butt of a machine gun. He collapsed to the floor of the truck, which lurched into motion. As they neared the northern end of the piazza, Federico saw two German soldiers on the sidewalk deep in conversation. He took action on instinct. He leapt from the truck, ran up to one of them, and said, "Fritz, wie geht's?" ("How's it going?") He actually hugged the soldier, who was so shocked, he stood back, slack-jawed. Federico used the moment to race off into the first street he saw. It was via Margutta.

The street was deserted. Federico looked frantically for someplace to hide. He had no idea whether anyone was behind him. He heard the sound of a metal gate creaking up. Halfway down the narrow street, a man was opening his pharmacy. He took one look at Federico. His face remained impassive. He waved Federico under the metal gate. Federico folded his lanky frame underneath. He was momentarily disoriented by the semi-darkness. For the second time that day he felt a hand at his back. It guided him toward a cellar door. Federico spent the day there.

Twice he heard the guttural sounds of German being spoken in the pharmacy; he couldn't tell whether they were searching it or just getting medication. The pharmacist brought Federico bread and cheese. They never spoke.

When darkness fell, the pharmacist opened the cellar door and waved Federico to the doorway. Federico began to go down via Margutta when the pharmacist grabbed him from behind and turned him the other way. Federico had just missed a German patrol. Federico would never forget the haunted eyes of the pharmacist, who said in a whisper as Federico began his walk home, "They took my son last month. I have never heard from him."

Federico's walk was filled with dread. When he arrived at the apartment, Giulietta broke down in tears. She clung to her new husband as if she would never let him go.

As theaters closed and film production all but ceased during the occupation, deprivations increased. Federico marveled at how Giulietta and her aunt kept order in the apartment and found something to put on the table to eat; often it was nothing more than broth. The winter was unusually cold and there was not enough coal to heat their apartment.

On March 3, 1944, Aldo Fabrizi appeared at their door. Federico had not seen him for a long time. Fabrizi's face was ashen. He lived in the neighborhood near viale Giulio Cesare. There were barracks on the street that were being used by the Germans to house prisoners who were on their way to labor camps. Fabrizi had witnessed a crowd of women who were protesting the treatment of their husbands, many of whom were prisoners slated for deportation. One woman, Maria Teresa Gullace, a pregnant mother of five, went near a window, presumably to give her imprisoned husband something to eat. A German soldier walked up to her and shot her in the head with a Luger. She had already become a martyr. Fabrizi was filled with anguish as he told the story of what he had seen.

Federico and Giulietta, sequestered for the most part in the apartment on via Lutezia, also heard rumors of sadistic tortures taking place at Nazi headquarters on via Tasso. There was a boys' school next door and they could hear the screams of the prisoners who were being tortured. One side of the headquarters had plush carpeting, a grand piano, and antique furniture. The other side was where the SS, headed by Colonel Kappler, conducted torture sessions. Resistance actions continued and escalated despite the threat of death. One priest, Don Morosini, was executed for his actions on behalf of the resistance.

On March 23, 1944, resistance operatives detonated a bomb in via Rasella that killed thirty-three German policemen. On hearing of the deaths, Hitler initially ordered the bombing of Rome. Ultimately Hitler left the reprisal to Field Marshall Albert Kesselring. The decision was to execute ten Italian men for every German who had been killed. Under orders from Kesselring, the SS rounded up 335 men from the prison on viale Giulio Cesare, as well as from a Jewish prison and, ultimately, from the streets. The youngest was fifteen. The oldest was in his late seventies. They were taken to the Ardeatine Caves on the outskirts of Rome and executed at close range with bullets to the back of the skull. The caves were then bombed to seal off the dead.

Federico, Giulietta, and Auntie believed everything they heard. They got their information from furtive visits by friends. They also heard the agonized screams of women and children who had lost their fathers and sons. Every Roman lived in fear of the sound of the marching boots and the guttural utterances of the Germans. The air raid sirens were becoming more frequent, yet because of Rome's architectural, historic, and religious significance, both sides had agreed not to destroy the city. Federico tried to reassure the women that the bombs were Allied attempts to destroy outlying factories and airfields. It was cold comfort. He did his best to convince them that soon the Americans would come and liberate their beloved city.

Riccardo, Federico's younger brother, burst into the via Lutezia apartment one day, red-faced and out of breath.

"Someone saw Yanks south of the city. They were coming from Anzio, from Cassino. This morning."

Outside on the street, Federico could see columns of German soldiers. But they were no longer conducting searches. They appeared to be in a hurry. A German truck rumbled down via Lutezia and the soldiers jumped up onto the sides, hanging on as it sped away.

"It's going north," Riccardo continued. "I tell you, they are leaving. They don't give a damn about Rome anymore. They are going to Florence—north, to fight. The Yanks have routed them." He disappeared down the stairs.

It was the morning of June 5, 1944, and Giulietta begged Federico to stay inside. But finally, around noon, they began to hear shouts and cheering. They were confused, as they had been told to stay indoors. But the tenor of the voices and the sight of people pouring out of doorways onto via Lutezia overcame any residual fear. Giulietta and Federico ran down the stairs leading to the street. They stood in the June sunshine looking at one another. They realized at the same moment that they were no longer under the control of the Fascist government. They were no longer bound by the shackles of German tyranny.

They stepped off the curb. They were nearly run over by a battered German tank. It was racing down the street, full of SS troops. They paid no attention to the increasing crowds in the streets. They were indeed headed north to Florence. The streams of astonished Romans seemed to be heading toward St. Peter's Square. Shopkeepers were closing up, waiters were throwing down their aprons, mothers and children were running, following the growing stream. Federico and Giulietta passed the Excelsior Hotel on via Veneto as two dazed German officers were scrambling outside. Behind them, a large American flag, hidden away for just such a moment, was being raised.

Federico held tightly to Giulietta's hand. They kept staring at each other as if to reassure themselves that this was not a dream. And then they saw it: An American tank was rolling down the street. Three young Roman women were clinging to the side. Two of them were being kissed by American soldiers. Federico stared in wonder at the Americans, whose faces were filthy. Some responded to the flowers being thrown at them. They grabbed the hands of well-wishers; they brought some of them up to the gun turret where they sat, girls in dresses with flowered patterns against the brown and green grime of the tanks. Federico also noticed other soldiers, who seemed not to know where they were. They stared straight ahead. The noise and cheering seemed not to affect them. Their faces were frozen. One simply disappeared into the body of the tank.

They passed Palazzo Venezia, Mussolini's former headquarters. The tanks were now being followed by jeeps. They made a snaking line as far as the eye could see. The gathering crowds surged around the Americans in a sea of cheering and screaming.

One wiry soldier jumped out of his jeep when it was directly in front of the Palazzo Venezia. He spoke Italian and asked to be hoisted up to the balcony over the front door. The crowd eagerly obeyed. He carried an American flag, which he attached to the balcony. He asked the crowd for quiet.

"I am Sergeant John Vita from Brooklyn and my mamma came from Reggio Calabria. She made me promise I would fly the stars and stripes from Mussolini's balcony." He unfurled the flag, saying, "This is for my mamma. Conquer! Conquer! Conquer!"

The crowd went wild. Once Vita had jumped down from the balcony, Federico forced his way to where the sergeant stood. Federico produced a napkin, on the back of which he quickly sketched a drawing of the soldier triumphantly standing on Mussolini's balcony. Sergeant Vita kissed a surprised Giulietta. Then he thanked Federico profusely. He insisted on paying for the drawing. He shoved a pile of American money into Federico's pocket and gave them two packages of American cigarettes. He said, "Grazie, grazie," as he was swept up in the crowd that was surging toward St. Peter's.

"There are going to be fifty thousand Yanks in this city before long," said one man, wiping his forehead with a handkerchief. "That's a lot of money and cigarettes."

Federico turned the cigarette package over and over in his hand, momentarily mesmerized by the design of the circle logo and the cellophane. He was impressed.

He turned to Giulietta and said, "If only we had seen this before the war, the Fascists would have known they'd never win."

Then they were swept up in the crowd that pushed toward St.

Peter's. The crush of people came upon lines of tanks, jeeps, and columns of American soldiers. Seeing it as a whole, Federico had to admit there was an impressive sort of freedom in their movement, even considering the confines of their military training; they had an innate blend of confidence and swagger that was intoxicating. They threw cigarettes, chocolate bars, packages of white bread, and cans of strange foods that were often consumed on the spot. Throngs of spectators cheered a jeep that contained General Mark Clark, the commander of the Fifth Army. People ran toward him and kissed the American flag that hung from his jeep. The front of the vehicle was covered with flowers.

Pope Pius XII appeared on the balcony of the Vatican amid the sound of ringing bells. He raised his hands and began, "In recent days we have trembled for the fate of the city. Today we rejoice because, thanks to the goodwill of both sides, Rome has been saved from the horror of war."

A roar went up from the crowd. It rippled over the beleaguered citizenry and sailed up to the blue skies over Rome.

Federico and Giulietta returned to their apartment on via Lutezia as the sun was coming up the following morning. They had stayed for the Pope's speech. Then they walked all over their beloved city. Over fifty thousand soldiers entered the city that day, marching past the Coliseum, the Forum, and even through the Jewish quarter near the Tiber River, where they saw hundreds of people who had been in hiding emerge and place signs on the ancient synagogue, hoping to reunite with loved ones. They saw partisans bombing Fascist enclaves and evacuations of radio stations and newspapers that had become Nazi strongholds.

They saw scenes of drunken celebration and debauchery. They treated themselves to drinks at the Café de Paris, a place where artists and intellectuals gathered, on via Veneto. They had spent their last cent, but a major in the U.S. Army was buying drinks for everyone. In appreciation, Federico drew the man's caricature with the Coliseum in the background on the back of a Café de Paris napkin. "I'll keep this forever," the major had said.

Federico lay in bed next to his exhausted wife. They shared a precious American cigarette together before Giulietta drifted off.

Federico began to dream. He went over scenes of the day. Then he leapt out of bed with a jolt. He had an idea.

A week later, with a group of his illustrator friends De Seta, Verdini, Camerini, Scarpelli, Majorana, Guasta, Attalo, and Migneco, Federico opened a shop on via Nazionale. The street had been built during the Risorgimento—the unification of Italy—to connect Stazione Termini with the center of the city. It was now teeming with American GIs who seemingly had pockets full of money to spend, extra food to barter, and a desire for something to send home. Federico's Funny Face Shop provided just that. For the equivalent of three dollars, the GIs would have a caricature drawn by one of the owner/illustrators. For an extra two dollars, they would make a small record with a greeting. Federico and his colleagues hired attractive young women to entertain the crowds of GIs who almost immediately lined up to get inside.

The Funny Face Shop was a success—so much so that four other locations around the city were opened. The main store, on via Nazionale, became a combination of Wild West saloon and nightclub, with customers socializing as they waited to get their drawings done. It was a high-spirited, chaotic place with occasional drunken brawls. Customers often tipped with American cigarettes, bottles of beer, bars of chocolate, or canned goods, the likes of which many Romans had never seen or tasted. Federico and his colleagues made money hand over fist.

Federico dutifully brought the earnings home to Giulietta, who kept careful accounts. It was a habit that was to continue throughout their lives. Federico had no sense of money or how to save it.

One night in mid-July, after a particularly long day at Funny Face, Federico climbed the stairs to the apartment in via Lutezia. He heard Giulietta humming. He opened the door and saw their wedding invitation leaning against a can of American food. The invitation featured two cupids with arrows that pointed to a cherubic baby. Federico looked at Giulietta, who was smiling the way she had smiled on the day they met. He hadn't seen that smile in a long time.

"They say this American Spam has lots of protein. That's good for growing babies," she said.

They dined on their mysterious meat, which they smothered in a marinara sauce, as they talked over names for their baby.

Federico worked ever-longer hours at Funny Face. The fifty thousand soldiers of the Fifth Army had swarmed into Rome, changing its tempo, lifting the scourge of fear, and sporadically providing its inhabitants with food. The black market still flourished and deprivation and starvation remained an ever-present issue during the summer of 1944. The war raged on in northern

Italy and across Europe. Refugees continued to pour into the city.

The Funny Face Shop became a refuge of sorts for writers and artists as well as for GIs. Cinecittà had been bombed during the Allied advance and now housed refugees. Screenwriters such as Cesare Zavattini, Ennio Flaiano, and Tullio Pinelli discussed ideas for films; they were full of stories and inspired by what was happening around them. Lux Film, a production company that had been formed by anti-Fascist Riccardo Gualino in 1934, and had employed many writers, was struggling to reinstate itself. There was no dearth of writers or ideas for stories. There was no lack of passion or desire to make films. But there was also no film stock. There were no studios. Electricity was still unreliable.

Federico, flush with the success of the Funny Face shops, was content, for the moment, to make money for his family. Although by 1944 he had contributed to over two dozen films as a script doctor, scenarist, and advisor, he still didn't consider himself a full-time filmmaker. On the other hand, he was acutely aware that eventually the soldiers would leave and the officers who replaced them to remain in Italy more permanently would not be the kind to patronize the Funny Face.

Federico continued, for the time being, to manage the Funny Face shops. He had an extra reason now for making them a success. There were more frequent fisticuffs, and the military police, headquartered conveniently around the corner, came so often they all knew Federico by name.

In September 1944, on a day when the shop was full because the soldiers had just gotten their pay, Federico sat on his stool finishing a caricature for an Asian soldier. The soldier was weaving back and forth, obviously drunk.

Federico spotted a slender man with an aquiline profile standing near the entrance. He wore a trench coat that had seen better days and a flop hat that shaded his eyes just enough to allow him to observe others without appearing to stare. Federico turned back to his woozy customer and realized with a start that he knew the man with the flop hat—it was Roberto Rossellini. They had met at the *Marc'Aurelio* offices and Federico recalled him fondly. He couldn't imagine what Rossellini was doing at Funny Face.

Federico quickly finished the drawing and gave it to his customer, who leapt up and quickly brandished a razor blade at Federico.

"You've made me yellow. You've made my skin yellow. Insult! Imbecile! Stupid!"

He tossed the stool he had been sitting on and came at Federico. The fistfight was on. The siren of the military police jeep was heard over the din. Rossellini appeared at Federico's side and handed him a stick of pink chalk. Federico quickly changed the hue of the skin on the caricature and stuck the drawing in the back pocket of the soldier as he was being loaded into the jeep, handcuffed.

Federico looked at Rossellini and shrugged. "He already paid for the drawing. Razor blade attack or not, I always satisfy my customers."

As Federico wiped his hands, Rossellini, who had been watching it all with a bemused air, said, "Why did I not know this before? This is clearly the most explosive and exciting place in all of Rome."

Federico laughed, turned over the stool that had been hurled at him moments before, and invited Rossellini to sit down.

"Just another day at the office," Federico said.

The man who sat before him had been born in Rome in 1906. He was fourteen years older than Federico. He was the eldest of three children and had grown up in a palazzo on the edge of Rome, where city met country. His grandfather was a builder and developer. His father was an architect. Roberto had grown up with great wealth and privilege in the midst of an eccentric, artistic family that spent money lavishly. The Rossellinis encouraged freedom of thought and the pursuit of all interests—political, artistic, intellectual, sexual. Roberto's mother was kind and loving, but frequently overwhelmed by the bohemian nature of the huge household.

His father was often either gone on business or involved in extramarital affairs. When he was home, he held nightly salons with Rome's great artists and philosophers. The children were not told to remain quiet; they were encouraged to perform songs and plays and to have and give their opinions about whatever was being discussed. It was impossible to know, on many nights, who might be a guest at their dinner table.

Rossellini was sickly in his childhood and loved nothing more than to lie in bed for days devouring novels by Flaubert, Dostoevsky, Stendhal, and Balzac. He despised school because he found it tedious. He loved the attention he got from his mother when he was sick. He developed into a stubborn, tenacious young man who was used to getting his way, but doing so with charm and wit. During the Spanish Flu of 1918, Roberto nearly lost his life. His mother prayed to God to let her son live. She vowed that she would wear black the rest of her life if God did so. When Roberto survived, she fudged and wore mauve, as it was more flattering; she simply assumed God wouldn't mind.

The wealthy class in Rome was not initially affected when Mussolini came into power in 1922. The Rossellini family watched with detached interest the bombastic speech from their home across the street from the Hotel Savoy, where Mussolini stood on the balcony declaiming his power and the greatness of the Fascist movement. Beppino Rossellini, Roberto's father, simply shrugged and said, "Remember, children, the color black is good for hiding dirt."

Beppino had designed and built the most modern cinema in all of Rome. It was called the Corso and even had a roof that retracted on summer nights. Roberto had free passes and made frequent use of them treating friends and seeing films over and over again. He revered Chaplin, D. W. Griffith, Murnau, and von Stroheim.

For most of his twenties Roberto was a profligate man-about-town, spending money wildly, dating a variety of beautiful women, and racing cars. It was still unusual to own a car and Rossellini had a red Bugatti. He alternated between deep, intellectual evenings in conversation and study and indulgence in alcohol and cocaine. Even his notoriously lenient bohemian father exploded with fury when Roberto, exhausted by drug use, was confined for a time to an institution. It prompted serious discussions with his father about the purpose of life. They shared a common interest in the philosopher Benedetto Croce, who believed that reliving or re-examining the past was an essential part of grasping the present; he believed that history and story were one. Croce's belief that looking at the past with art and imagination would bring renewal became a tenet of Rossellini's own personal ethos.

On March 6, 1931, when Roberto was twenty-five years old, his father died suddenly at the age of fifty. The three Rossellini children were soon to discover that there was no more money. The inheritance had been spent. Roberto, who had both loved and rebelled against his father, realized that he had to begin to work for a living. He had a wife and a child on the way. He found work at Cinematografica Italiana arranging dubbing for American films. Eventually he began working with Vittorio Mussolini, the son of Benito, writing films. The first was *Luciano Serra,* a film on which he was working when Cinecittà opened in 1937. He also made a documentary film about the life of insects. Three films for which he became well known were propaganda for the Italian Army, Navy, and Air Force.

By the time the war broke out, he had a reputation as a competent filmmaker. He was successful and well known by the film community; he was appreciated for his intelligence, wit, and charm. He had two sons, a wife, and a German mistress whose background came in handy at the beginning of the war. But even her influence could not help Rossellini when Mussolini was deposed and Rome was occupied. With the Nazi occupation of Rome, Rossellini became a hunted man like all men of military age. He moved from house to house nightly and was nearly caught more than once. The feeling of constant terror was seared into his memory. It would propel him to find ways to express this on film in the coming years.

Despite the need to hide, Rossellini and fellow artists met secretly at apartments all over Rome. One writer, Sergio Amidei, who had been born in Trieste in 1904 and had begun his career as an actor, had become a respected screenwriter. Amidei and Rossellini began to meet and discuss ideas for a film. They wanted to tell the stories of the struggles Romans and the Italian people had endured in the recent past. They felt they had a specific history they wanted to share with the world. It was a story they didn't see portrayed in any other movie. Rossellini and Amidei finally arrived at the notion of combining two stories: the execution of the priest Don Morosini and the shooting of Maria Teresa Gullace. Amidei conceived it as a moral story, a cry of revenge against injustice and tyranny. Rossellini was more interested in human behavior and depicting the lives of actual Romans during the occupation, the terror and fear that had shaped their lives.

Rossellini began the arduous task of producing the film. He found a countess who was willing to put up some money. She wanted to be reassured there would be stars in the film to ensure its success. Amidei continued to work on the script. There remained the question of finding an actor to play Don Morosini. Aldo Fabrizi was perfect for the role. His stature and popularity would legitimize the project. He was known and beloved by both theater and film audiences. He was a consummate actor who could play the comedic everyman as well as express the sorrow and pain of his characters.

At a dinner during the summer of 1944, Amidei and Rossellini began to tell him the story of the film. Fabrizi burst into tears and told them he had actually witnessed the killing of Maria Teresa Gullace, and that he would love to do the film. Rossellini and Amidei were thrilled. Fabrizi got up from the table, thanked them for dinner, and then added, "For a million lire." He turned on his heel and left the restaurant.

That sum was more than the entire budget of the film. But they had to have Fabrizi. Someone would have to talk him out of three-fourths of the salary he had demanded. Amidei remembered that Federico Fellini and Fabrizi were the best of friends, and Rossellini seized on the idea of asking Federico to intercede. But he knew that in order to make the ask, he would have to offer Federico something. Clearly, it would have to be work on the film.

Rossellini began his pitch to Federico by complimenting the younger man on his writing. He invited Federico to the Caffè Castellino after the Funny Face Shop closed for the night. He outlined the story, the themes they wanted to explore, and the idea of shooting the film in the actual locations, or near the actual locations, where some of the events had happened. He explained the dilemma with Fabrizi and finished by inviting Federico to work on the script.

"I'm not fooled into thinking that he leapt at the chance to have me as a writer," said Federico as he lay next to his wife that night. "I know he is desperate for Fabrizi. But he's offering me a job as a writer, so why not take advantage?"

"The second wave of Americans, the ones who are coming now, are officers. They aren't the types who are going to patronize the Funny Face Shop. Fefe, this is a chance," said Giulietta.

"A countess is financing it . . . there is no film stock, no daytime electricity, no studio, and no distribution plan. Nothing is certain."

"Nothing is ever certain, love. We have to follow our hearts."

"He did offer me 25,000 lire, so that's good."

Giulietta laughed and paused for a long moment. "As I said, nothing is ever certain. But we do it anyway . . . for love, for life, for chance. You must say yes, Fefe."

Amidei and Federico began meeting in the apartment on via Lutezia. Giulietta had passed her first trimester and was feeling the warm glow of a pregnant woman. She was energized by the script conferences and glad to see Federico engaged in writing. Federico did indeed convince his good friend Aldo Fabrizi to accept the role for a much lower salary. Aldo Fabrizi was persuaded because he was made comfortable by Federico's involvement. He felt that Federico, who had been raised in a working-class family in Emilia-Romagna, understood his idioms better than Amidei, who had been raised in Trieste.

Shooting began on January 17, 1945. A small makeshift studio on via degli Avignonesi had been set up. It was situated directly below a bordello. The production had to shoot at night because electricity was so scarce during the day. Rossellini spent part of his time on the phone in the caffè next door, desperately soliciting financing for the production.

In the ensuing months, Federico had ample opportunity to observe Rossellini at work. He juggled directing the film, raising the money, and dealing with a wife, two children, a mistress, and occasional affairs with actresses in the film. He nurtured and tended to the ego needs of his two stars, one of whom was Aldo Fabrizi. The other, playing the role of Maria Teresa Gullace, named Pina Sora in the film, was the volatile actress Anna Magnani.

Magnani had been abandoned by her mother as a toddler. She was raised in a convent and found escape in music and acting. A force of nature, Magnani used her personal pain and agony to create searing and unforgettable cinematic moments. She was a deeply loyal friend and came to rely on Rossellini's empathy during the filming, particularly when her own son had to be hospitalized with polio. If she was crossed, however, her rage boiled over with an intensity that was both frightening and singular. Once, when her lover visited the set unexpectedly, Magnani lashed out at him, accusing him of infidelity. They had a fistfight. He tried to escape. Cast and crew watched as Magnani ran after him, screaming and attacking him from behind.

Federico was amazed to see Rossellini observing all this human behavior with a calm and detached air. By this time, Federico had seen enough of Rossellini to know that interesting things that happened on set would often as not make their way into the film. Federico was certain this incident would somehow appear in the movie, which was now called *Rome, Open City.*

Rossellini didn't work like other directors. He would let scenes go on for several minutes without cutting. He didn't want the actors to be interrupted. Even when they made mistakes or forgot their lines, he often refused to do retakes; he felt that natural human behavior and the responses between the actors were more important than trying to make a point with camera moves and cuts. Amidei, who wanted each scene to be directed to make a point, was often frustrated by this.

Federico made himself indispensable during the shoot. He was affable and witty and befriended the entire crew and cast. He observed the differences between Amidei and Rossellini with interest. Rossellini, at thirty-eight, became a kind of father figure to Federico and impressed the younger man with his ability to remain calm and unperturbed during even the most harried situations. It almost felt to Federico as if Rossellini created them, thrived on them, as though they were the creative juices that fed what happened on camera. The line between what happened on camera and what happened off camera sometimes grew imperceptible.

On March 22, 1945, Federico was called from the set of *Rome, Open City* to Santo Spirito Hospital. Auntie stood outside, beckoning Federico to the obstetrics floor. Giulietta was asleep. Beside her, wrapped in swaddling, was a tiny baby boy with a shock of dark hair. He was restless, reaching his tiny hand up to the outside of his white linen wrap.

"You are not content to be bound up in that thing, are

you?" Federico said to his new son. "You are my Pierfederico; like father, like son."

During the two weeks that followed, Giulietta suffered from abdominal pain and fever. Pierfederico, despite constant attention, was alternately listless and inconsolable. He was limp and lethargic at times. At times he would scream through the night. Giulietta insisted that Federico go to the set of *Rome, Open City*. She believed he belonged there and encouraged him to continue working.

"Auntie and I can handle your son; he just has an artistic temperament," said Giulietta.

They had nearly finished shooting one night in mid-April. Rossellini had befriended an American journalist who stole precious film stock for the director from his office; Rossellini had also sold his own furniture, watches, and other jewelry to make payroll. Typical of Rossellini, the precarious finances always seemed on the verge of drying up, but the intrepid director somehow found a way. An American soldier named Rod Geiger had befriended Rossellini. He had seen parts of the film and recognized Rossellini was creating something unseen before, a new kind of cinema. He had a line on American distribution for the film.

Federico was anxious to get home to his wife and son. The sun was just rising. He saw Auntie making her way to the set. She had never come to the set and wouldn't do so unless something terrible had happened. She was ashen.

When they arrived at Santo Spirito, it was nearly dawn. Giulietta was holding Pierfederico. He was not moving.

"We have lost him to encephalitis, Fefe. The doctor says I can't have any more children, Fefe. What will we do? Will you still love me?"

Federico held her, and his son. They stood like that, frozen in grief, until Auntie came to lead them home.

April 21, 1945, was one of the final days of shooting *Rome, Open City*. Federico had contributed a scene in which an old man is banged on the head with a frying pan so as not to alert Nazis to the whereabouts of a gun. The actors had performed it perfectly and they were now on to the final scene for that day. Extras dressed in Nazi uniforms (actually department of sanitation uniforms with fake SS belt buckles) stood outside. The ever-present crowd of onlookers confused reality with filmmaking. Many of them had husbands and sons who were still fighting. The sight of Nazi soldiers on the street just four months after the real ones had departed incensed the crowd. Amidei passionately explained that this was a film, they were actors, and that it was their chance to tell the world about what they had all suffered under the hands of the Germans. Federico watched as Rossellini remained calm and unperturbed.

Moments later, "action" was called. Anna Magnani burst through a doorway and ran after the truck into which the actor playing her husband had been thrown. Two shots were heard and she fell in the middle of the street, executed by the SS. The actor playing her child ran after her and burst into tears. The scene was so realistic and disturbing that the child actor could not be comforted; he kept screaming and crying. Magnani, who had performed the scene full out, had fallen to the street on her knees. They were both bleeding.

Federico watched in complete absorption and horror, knowing it was unreal and yet real. He staggered into an alleyway where no one could see him. He had not been able to cry about his son. He had been strong for Giulietta. Now he fell to his knees and sobbed uncontrollably. His wails were echoed in the wet stone. Waves of misery seemed to rack his being. Then he felt a pair of strong arms surround him. It was Anna Magnani. She took his head onto her lap and rocked back and forth.

"I have known tragedy. My son Lucca had polio. If something happened to him . . . ." Tears poured down her cheeks. "You poor man. Poor man. Poor father."

They sat like that in the alleyway until they could cry no more. Then they got up and went back to work.

Federico and Giulietta wanted to be alone in their grief. They found comfort in walking all over the city—their beloved Rome. They walked past the former Nazi headquarters on via Tasso. They walked through the San Lorenzo district that had been bombed. They walked to the Portico d'Ottavia, the Jewish quarter, where they saw that their favorite tortoise fountain had been restored. Inhabitants had removed the bronze tortoises during the occupation. Now the water trickled down the shells as the bronze gleamed in the sun.

Giulietta touched them and looked up at Federico. "For good luck."

They sat near the cobblestone entrance and looked out at

the Tiber. Photos of lost family members still clung to the walls of the quarter; they had been there since the liberation.

"There has been so much death here," she said. "No one has been untouched by it. We have to create our life, the life we want to live. We can't live in the past."

"Rossellini has a way of taking the past but making it live in the present, making it inform the present. He is making another film. The one he really wants to make. About all of Italy, the things it has suffered. He wants me to work on it. He has a role for you."

"Is that our purpose in life, Fefe?" asked Giulietta.

"My purpose is to get to the Castellino as soon as possible. They run out of the lasagna ricotta early in the day." He took his wife's hand. He looked at her and saw himself reflected in the dark depth of her warm brown eyes. "Our work and what we create will be our children, what we leave behind."

Giulietta and Federico attended the premiere of *Rome, Open City* together. It was proclaimed as a new kind of cinema: neo-realism. Myths grew up around the term; various journalists claimed that all the actors were non-professional, that all the locations were real, that much of it was improvised. None of that was true. Actors like Aldo Fabrizi and Anna Magnani were seasoned professionals. Screenwriters had labored over the scripts and stories. Many scenes in *Rome, Open City* were shot in the makeshift studio below the bordello. But the deep feelings of terror and the agony of existence during an occupation were real. Many of the actors onscreen had felt and witnessed the injustices they were portraying. In making *Rome, Open City,* Roberto Rossellini and his colleagues elevated the tragedy of the recent past to a new art form that allowed their fellow countrymen and women to bathe in the city's sorrow and its hope. Don Morosini's final lines, "It is not hard to die a good death. It is hard to live a good life," seemed to both sum up the terrible sacrifice of the past and provide guidance for a better future.

Federico continued to work as a screenwriter for Lux Film, which produced commercial product, as well as to develop his own ideas for screenplays. Rossellini, with the backing of Rod Geiger, the American film entrepreneur, began preparing for a second film, *Paisan,* that would focus on the war in Italy as the Allies made their way up the Italian peninsula from Sicily. He asked Federico to be not only a writer, but also an assistant director.

Paisan centered around themes of miscommunication and coping with different cultures as the American forces came into contact with various kinds of people on the Italian peninsula: Neapolitans, Sicilians, Florentines, monks, primitive villagers, and partisans in the Po Valley. The film had six different episodes that took place in distinctly different locales. They began in the tiny town of Maiori on the Amalfi coast. Maiori was a fishing village that in many ways hadn't changed since ancient times. Federico discovered a monastery near Maiori that became the story of one of the episodes in the film. They moved to Naples, where Federico explored the slum lives of poor Neapolitans and came to know the suffering they had endured during the war.

In Florence they filmed where some fighting was still going on. They finished in the Po Valley.

Federico had the opportunity to work closely with Rossellini. Rossellini's belief that life around the film set was nearly equal to the drama that was being filmed appealed to Federico. Rossellini's ability to remain calm in the midst of chaos and his insistence on finding the deep truth in the stories he wanted to tell made an indelible impression on the younger man. Amidei and other writers often said they didn't like going to sets; they found them places of chaos. Federico discovered that he loved sets. He loved the actors, the personal dramas, the interplay between reality and fantasy. Federico had not traveled much in his own country and the making of *Paisan* gave him the opportunity to see firsthand how the war had affected his countrymen.

One night, while shooting the final episode of *Paisan* in the Po River Valley, a place Rossellini knew well from childhood, Federico found the director in his small hut. It was the middle of the night—Federico's favorite time. The cast and crew were sequestered in rustic living quarters while shooting the sequence that took place on the Po River. Rossellini was so absorbed in what he was doing that he didn't hear Federico. He was bent over, editing the previous day's work. He stared intently through the viewfinder.

He looked up at Federico, finally, and his eyes were shining. "It's so beautiful, isn't it?"

Federico understood what "it" was. The scene, the film, the story they were telling, the life they were leading. Federico had to admit that, yes, it was beautiful. He knew at that moment how he wanted to spend the rest of his life. He too would tell stories. In his own way. He would dream his own dreams with cinema.

Giulietta shot her first scene on film as the daughter of a major in the Florence episode of *Paisan.* They used the steps of Auntie Giulia's apartment for the location. Later that day, Rossellini, who had to placate his current mistress, asked Federico to take over for him. It was a scene in which partisans are dragging a water bottle across a road. The director of photography wanted to shoot from above. Federico insisted it be shot from the point of view of the street. It was his first time directing. He would not relent. He got his way.

"How does it feel to be a film actress?" he asked Giulietta that night, after the cables had been rolled up, the cameras packed away, and the cast and crew dispersed.

"The same way it feels to be a screenwriter and a director," she said, her eyes shining. "Seeing your dreams come to life. I feel alive, Fefe."

On March 13, 1947, Federico found he had been nominated, along with Sergio Amidei, for an Academy Award as a screenwriter for *Rome, Open City.* In Rimini, he never dreamed of such a thing. But Rome had given birth to new dreams. Those dreams were to be shared. This is what Rossellini did. He had the talent to invite the artists around him to share in the passion of his vision, the expression of life as Italians really lived, their suffering and their joy. Rossellini told his stories with the courage of his convictions. In so doing, he created a whole new kind of cinema. Federico had absorbed it all. He was ready to share his own dreams and visions.

Chapter Five

THE DREAM OF DIRECTING

Federico stopped by the news kiosk on via Veneta, as he did every evening. As a former journalist, he had honed the skill of skimming the paper and gleaning the important items. Why waste money on a purchase? The June 1946 election was a month away and the political battle over monarchy versus democracy filled the front page. Federico towered over a man who stood directly in front of him. He was also avidly skimming the headlines.

Feeling the presence of Federico behind him, the shorter man turned and said, "Ready for page two? Although I can already tell you it's not going to turn out well for the monarchy. Except in my own household. My wife is the queen. My four children rule me. And I am the court jester."

Federico smiled. "You are the great Tullio Pinelli. I recognize you from Lux. I've seen you talking to the bigwigs. I'm just a humble gag writer. I'm too shy to say hello."

"Gag writers don't get nominated for Academy Awards," answered Pinelli. "You are Fellini, and former owner of Funny

Face. I tried to get in once, but was mowed down by three drunken GIs. Which way are you walking? I can tell you everything you need to know in that paper. The world is still going to hell. The rich are evil. The young are crazy."

"I'm going home, to my three-room mansion on via Lutezia where I live with my wife and her aunt," said Federico. "My servant—meaning me—will be happy to share yesterday's gnocchi and a glass or two of rotgut wine, which is all we can afford right now."

The two men began walking toward Federico's apartment. Tullio Pinelli was twelve years older than Federico. He was descended from Piedmontese patriots. He was a lawyer who had spent his twenties in civil courtrooms. Pinelli lived a double life. At the same time he was arguing cases, he became fascinated with the theater. He began to write plays. Some were based on myths and ancient stories and some reflected current affairs. All were suffused with Pinelli's cool observance of human behavior and clear-eyed storytelling. His plays began to be produced in Turin as early as 1932. One in particular, *Battle With an Angel,* caught the eye of Guido Gatti, the head of Lux Film. Gatti was always on the lookout for great writers. He invited the Turinese lawyer-turned-playwright to work on an adaptation of an Alexander Pushkin novel for the screen. It was successful at the box office. From there, Pinelli's career as a screenwriter took off. He was married with four children. After spending several years going back and forth between Turin and Rome, he had recently moved his family permanently to Rome.

Pinelli was slightly detached, wry, and witty. His lawyer's

training allowed him to retain an air of perpetual observant interest. He was alert to the sensibility and behaviors of everyone he met; they were all, to him, fodder for a story. Federico struck Pinelli immediately as an unusually brilliant, charming young man with a poetic take on life that was different, though complementary, to his own.

The two men walked to the apartment on via Lutezia. Pinelli met Giulietta, who was impressed by the screenwriter's quiet, calm manner, so different from the actors she was accustomed to meeting. She went to bed while the men sat up talking, nearly until dawn. They discussed their personal and artistic lives. They came up with an outline for a film about a simple office worker who discovers that he can fly. The idea was never made into a screenplay. But the relationship formed that night was the basis for a writing partnership that lasted nearly two decades.

They found a desk at Lux in which they sat opposite one another. During the first part of the day, they worked together on scripts for producers at Lux. In the afternoon, they worked on their own ideas. Tullio Pinelli gave Federico structure and grounding. Federico gave Pinelli a sense of poetry, mysticism, and fantasy. Their subjects and interest often strayed from the neo-realistic, tragic, postwar subject matter that had occupied much of Federico's previous work with Rossellini. Gatti and other producers at times provided the two writers with money to research the films they asked them to write. These research trips led to bonding between the two artists as they explored Naples, Venice, and Trieste, and even a cathedral in Cologne, Germany. The experiences Pinelli and Federico had together laid the groundwork for the long collaboration they were to have. Although the screenplays they produced for Lux had varying degrees of success, the professional experience solidified their relationship as well as their reputation in the burgeoning postwar cinema world. It also taught them to work in the world of commercial film.

Alberto Lattuada, born in Vaprio d'Adda, Italy, was a director and screenwriter Federico came to know at Lux Film. Lattuada came from a literary background and had studied to be an architect to please his father, but the art of screenwriting drew him to Rome and Lux. In 1947, when he met Federico, Lattuada was already established as a writer and had directed several films. He was also married to the beautiful and successful film actress Carla Del Poggio.

Lattuada hired Pinelli and Federico to write the screenplay for *Without Pity,* a film about an interracial romance set in the gritty port town of Livorno. It explores the relationship between a black American soldier and a young Italian woman forced into prostitution. The young woman was played by Carla Del Poggio. *Without Pity* was a milestone experience for Federico. Many of the people who worked on that film became his colleagues for years to come.

Like Pinelli, Lattuada immediately saw Federico's unique ability to bring life and passion to whatever he did. It became increasingly clear that Pinelli, the quiet ex-lawyer, enjoyed writing, but had no desire to be near the set. Federico, on the other hand, seemed to come alive when on set. He enjoyed the actors and the crew, and became a general problem solver during the *Without Pity* shoot. If it was raining, he quickly rewrote the script to reflect that. He stood in for crew members who got ill. He spoke with nervous producers. He put the actors at ease. Federico took note of the difference between Rossellini, who tended to stay on the sidelines and observe what happened, and Lattuada, who got right into the middle of things. Both directors, Federico observed, seemed to share a love of an atmosphere of noise and chaos; they seemed to thrive on it and it fed them creatively.

As preparations for *Without Pity* were underway at Lux Film, Federico found a compact man with a briefcase standing in front of the offices one day. Federico asked him what he was waiting for. He replied simply that he was the composer for *Without Pity,* that his name was Nino Rota, and that he was waiting for a bus. Federico explained that there was no bus that came to where the composer was waiting. Rota insisted calmly that the bus would come. Federico had never seen a bus anywhere near the spot. But he was impressed by the man's confidence and decided to wait with him. It was a misty, dark evening. And sure enough, a bus seemed to appear out of nowhere.

Federico often thought back to this evening and this initial meeting. They worked together for nearly thirty years, two artists who seemed to share a special language. They seemed to understand one another intrinsically and, as the bus had come out of nowhere, they seemed to conjure from one another artistic magic.

Nino Rota was a composer born in 1911 in Milan. He had been a prodigy who came from a musical family. He wrote his first oratorio at age eleven and had performed his compositions in Milan and Paris by the time he was thirteen. From 1930 to 1932, Rota went to the Curtis Institute in Philadelphia, where he learned conducting. When he moved back to Italy, he began teaching and composing at the Liceo Musicale in Bari. He also had a degree in literature. By the time he met Federico in 1948, he had already composed scores for thirty-two films. He was prolific, humble, and understated despite his great talent.

Federico felt immediately at ease with Rota. They seemed to speak the same language of intuition. Federico was fascinated by the way in which Rota used American spirituals for the score of *Without Pity.* Although Federico was not a trained musician and could not read notes, he always responded deeply to the simple beauty of Rota's melodies. The composer once said to Federico, "I can never quite reconcile the fact that I live in a world where there is so much unhappiness. If my music can give people just a moment of happiness, that is why I do it."

The designer for *Without Pity* was Piero Gherardi, a former architect-turned-costumer, set designer, and location scout who was born in Poppi, Italy. Federico appreciated Gherardi's love of improvisation and his ability to make use of whatever bits of costume or ephemera he happened to find on location. He had an eye for the unusual and, like Federico, was undeterred by the inevitable problems that arose on set; they seemed to help his creativity flower.

Clemente Fracassi, the producer for *Without Pity,* also saw in Federico someone whose stamina, charm, and utter dedication not only to the making of the film, but also to the life lived while doing so made him indispensable as well as highly desirable. Federico was the first to arrive on the set and often the last to leave. During the shoot, Federico could always be depended on to lift the spirits of the cast and crew.

"Do you ever go home?" Fracassi once asked Federico after a fourteen-hour day had been spent shooting at the port of Livorno.

Federico turned to him with a broad smile. "This is my home."

Giulietta was cast in *Without Pity* as the Livorno prostitute and best friend of the lead, Carla Del Poggio. Her character's determination, love for her friend, and the heartbreaking goodbye as she leaves for America touched audiences to the core. She won a Silver Ribbon at the Venice Film Festival in 1948 for her performance. During one wrenching scene, her character bonds with Del Poggio's character, who tells the story of losing her baby. Giulietta had not wanted to go the set that day.

"I know the reason why," said Federico.

Giulietta burst into tears. They rarely discussed Pierfederico. It was too painful.

"But you must do it," he continued. "You must do it for all of the women who have experienced this. That is why you are an actress. To bear their pain. To let them know they are not alone. To give them some sense that despite the pain and the loss, life can go on."

Federico's relationship with Rossellini was still vital. Rossellini, who had begun a tempestuous relationship with Anna Magnani, had agreed to find a cinematic vehicle that would display all her talents. He had made a film based on a Jean Cocteau monologue that featured only Magnani, but it was too short for an entire evening. He begged Federico to come up with an idea for a second film to round out the bill.

On a spring day in 1948, Rossellini, Federico, and Pinelli sat at a table in the Borghese Gardens discussing, as they always did, ideas for a film. In this case, it was the one for Magnani. Rossellini was getting desperate as Magnani had a short window in which she was available to film. Federico tossed out a tale he remembered from his childhood in Gambettola.

"What about the story of a woman who is a simple-minded goatherd who sees a wanderer and mistakes him for a saint? She has a child by him and claims it was immaculate conception."

Rossellini jumped on the idea, and within weeks, the script had been written. Then he insisted that Federico play the role of the wanderer. He also insisted that Federico dye his hair blond for the part. Rossellini had to be his most seductive, charming self to convince Federico to go through with it, but once cast, Federico committed to it. He endured endless teasing. But he traveled to the ancient town of Maiori, where they had filmed *Paisan,* to perform the wordless role opposite Magnani.

"Everyone on earth should be an actor for a day," he told Giulietta. "You are spoiled and treated like a baby with people to do things for you, get your coffee, light your cigarette."

Giulietta rolled her eyes. "Rossellini is only doing that to placate you, blondie."

The film, *The Miracle,* had modest success. It was most notable because it prompted a case that went to the Supreme

Court. The American Catholic Church wanted to stop distribution of the film on the grounds that it was morally objectionable. The American distributor, Joseph Burstyn, refused to accept this judgment. The case ultimately went to the Supreme Court and ended up in a victory for Burstyn, dealing a heavy blow to censorship. This ruling was to have reverberations that significantly altered the kinds of films that could be made and seen both in Europe and in America.

For his part, Federico was paid for his work on the film not in *lire,* but with a gift from Rossellini: a brand-new red Fiat Topolino. Federico loved nothing more than to drive late at night with a friend to Ostia or Fregene or along the Appia Antica, discussing story ideas, listening to the waves crash onto the beach, or seeing the ancient buildings and monuments flash by. "It is a kind of film all in itself," he mused.

On June 8, 1948, Rossellini received a letter that was to ultimately have reverberations around the world. It was simple enough: a straightforward note that complimented his work and offered the services of the letter writer, should he be interested. The writer was the world-renowned recipient of three nominations for an Academy Award for Best Actress and one win. Ingrid Bergman was, at the time, one of the most famous faces in the world. Rossellini lost no time in bringing her to Italy. They fell in love almost instantly, although both were already married. The scandal made constant headlines around the world and provided fodder for endless fan speculation. Giulietta and Federico welcomed the actress and socialized with the famous couple frequently. Rossellini asked Federico to continue to work with him, most particularly on the last of three films he made starring Bergman. *Europa '51* featured her as a society woman who turns to charity work after her own child dies. Giulietta was promised a large supporting role as a laborer who takes in orphans.

As part of engaging French producers to invest in the film, Rossellini took Federico on a trip to Paris. It was Federico's first time in the famed city. Sequestered with a group of intellectuals, Federico soon became bored and disenchanted. He found Paris to be precious and "presented," as though every site were in a picture book. He also found the snobbery of the elite both intimidating and nauseating. He left Paris early. He arrived home late at night. He had never been so happy to see Termini Station.

"Did you see the Eiffel Tower, Notre-Dame, the Champs-Élysées?" asked Giulietta, surprised to see her husband arrive home three days early.

She had been preparing assiduously, as she always did, for her role in *Europa '51*. She secretly hoped there hadn't been a rift between Federico and Rossellini.

"Paris is like a stage set for an overwrought fairy tale. Rome is like a comfortable apartment, with hallways and endless rooms to welcome and comfort you." Federico stretched out as best he could on their tiny bed. "Rossellini has taught me to live in the world of film, to embrace every aspect of it, to take the reality of the world into the unreality of film. But we come from different sensibilities and backgrounds. I don't want to make messages. The trip made me see that. I'm going to make a film with Lattuada. We are co-directing. It won't be about war or death. It will be about variety theaters."

Giulietta sat up in bed and leaned on her elbow. Her husband now took up more space. He had gained weight. He was no longer the skinny boy she had married. He gazed off into space, a million miles away. His feet still hung over the edge of the bed. *Why have we never bought a big enough bed?* she thought.

Federico lay there. His eyes were wide open. They were shining in the dark. He brought with him the smells of Rome: the lemony aftershave he used, the sweat from a long train ride, the espresso she knew he had imbibed at the Rosati. His writing pad was on his chest, his sketch pad on the floor next to his side, with colored pencils at the ready. She knew he would be awake for hours.

"Will there be a part for me?" she asked, yawning and pretending to be indifferent.

Federico kissed her forehead. "Ever the actress."

Federico and Tullio Pinelli came up with the idea for *Variety Lights* based on their mutual love for the kind of lowbrow theater that was fast fading from the Italian landscape. They brought in another writer, Ennio Flaiano, whom they knew from Lux. Flaiano was then forty, a deeply intellectual playwright, novelist, and critic. He had a biting, caustic wit and suffered no fools. He tended to be forthright about his opinions, unafraid to express them.

Born in Pescara on March 5, 1910, Flaiano was a well-established writer when he met Federico. His novel *A Time to*

Kill was the single literary effort to uncover the folly of the invasion of Ethiopia and expose its true tragedy. It won a coveted Strega Prize and catapulted Flaiano to the upper ranks of Italian intelligentsia. Flaiano thought deeply about his subjects and took political risks with his work. He shared with Federico a love of his adopted city, Rome. He was also quick to point out its vices as well as its virtues. Flaiano was particularly disparaging of the waste of war and the excesses of the burgeoning bourgeoisie in postwar Italy.

The triumvirate of Federico Fellini, Tullio Pinelli, and Ennio Flaiano, with their distinctive viewpoints and talents, would merge in one form or another for the next fifteen years and create the screenplays for some of the most memorable films ever made.

Federico could not have been more different in personality or background from Alberto Lattuada, the man with whom he co-directed *Variety Lights*. Lattuada came from a cultured, educated family and hired many of them to work on the film. His father wrote the score, his sister was the accountant, his wife was the star. Federico was from a working-class background, and read newspapers and comic books along with the occasional foray into Kafka. The atmosphere on the set was lighthearted and engaging, with Lattuada focusing on the technical elements and Federico on acting nuances and the detail of the sets and costumes. The director of photography, Otello Martelli, specialized in soft focus for actresses that made them luminous and gave depth and definition to the look and feel of the film.

Martelli became a permanent colleague of Federico's, beginning with *Variety Lights*.

Federico created an environment of freedom, and the cast and crew reflected the sense of fun and camaraderie. The film expressed simultaneously a love for the tawdry world of a traveling theater, the family it created offstage, and the illusions it created onstage.

When it premiered on December 16, 1950, *Variety Lights* received an underwhelming response. Some critics, in fact, were scathing. But others, such as producer Luigi Rovere, saw something special and monolithic in the scenes of a lonely plaza at night and the bedraggled procession of actors trudging down a country road. Rovere decided to offer Fellini a film to direct on his own: *The White Sheik*.

Federico stood just outside the front door of his apartment in a light coat and a black beret. The beret was perched at the back of his head, as if it were an afterthought. It was early October, 1951, and the leaves on the plane tree outside their window were just beginning to change color. Federico turned toward his wife, who was standing in the doorway to the apartment. The sun was just coming up and she wiped the sleep from her eyes. He hugged her with all his might. Giulietta could feel his heart pounding.

"You've got to let go. Get started. You'll be late," she said.

"Why did I ever agree to do this? To sign up for this madness? Whoever thought I could direct a film on my own?" Federico whispered. His eyes were wide with terror.

Giulietta hooted. "You did. You've been convincing people of it for months. You've insisted on every actor, gotten your way on every detail. You know that you are ready. Don't be silly."

"I wish you were coming with me," Federico said.

"If you'd given me a larger part, I would be," she said drily. She reached up to his shoulders, pulled him down, and kissed his forehead. "Stop into a church along the way. Pray. Now go." She watched him rush down the stairs, two at a time. "And don't eat too much pasta at lunch. You'll get sluggish." Giulietta laughed to herself. Federico had never in his life been sluggish.

Federico stopped into the Chigi Chapel just off Piazza del Popolo. He pushed at the door and it swung open with a loud creak. There was a single candle lighting something he couldn't see. Then he realized it was a coffin. He raced away.

The first day of shooting was in Fregene, a beach town just outside Rome. Federico was already an hour late. His tire blew. He was frantic. A truck driver with a load of chickens pulled over. The driver seemed to sense the need to move quickly. They replaced the tire. Chicken feathers flew.

Federico drove frantically onto the beach. He saw the crew on one boat, just offshore, and the two stars, Alberto Sordi and Brunella Bovo, floating on a boat next to the crew. They turned to stare at Federico in unison. Federico began to wade into the water. A production assistant stopped him and brought a boat. He stepped inside. The rest of the day was spent trying to film in a boat on the rolling sea. It did not go well. At day's end, Federico realized that the way to get the shot was to set up the camera on shore.

He spent that evening walking the streets of Rome. He returned to the Chigi Chapel. The coffin was gone. Now he could see the painting of the benevolent Madonna. It was lit by the setting sun. Federico was confident the second day would be glorious.

The next day, Federico brought to the set the lighthearted sense of fun he himself had enjoyed on other sets. Suddenly, he felt at ease. He knew where to place the camera and how to think ahead to coming shots. He knew exactly what he wanted out of each moment and each performance. He was overjoyed with the casting of Leopoldo Trieste, a playwright and sometime dramatic actor whom Federico believed would make a brilliant comedian. They became lifelong friends, and *Variety Lights* helped Trieste begin a thirty-year career as a sought-after character actor.

The theme of reality versus illusion underscored the story, which was based on the popular *fumetti,* or photographic film strips. They were published in the newspapers and could also be bought in magazine form. Easily understood by both literate and illiterate readers, they were comic soap operas with real photos.

The White Sheik follows the story of two rubes who come to Rome for their honeymoon. The husband has plans for his new wife to meet his family and ultimately the pope himself. The wife has another agenda. She is a fanatical fan of the *fumetti* hero the White Sheik and has drawn a picture for him. She escapes the honeymoon suite to pursue her hero and gets caught up in an actual film shoot in which her sheik is the star. Her husband, wracked with worry about his missing wife, has adventures on his own. Finally, both characters realize that they must adjust their fantasies to fit the new reality of their life.

For Federico, directing the film felt as though he had finally come home from a journey he didn't realize he had begun. He felt so comfortable in the world of filmmaking. He loved the off-camera life, the camaraderie, the set lunches, the extraordinary collaborations with fellow artists, the romantic intrigues that seemed to swirl around a film set. It all fed him and nurtured him.

He finished editing the film in March 1951 and set up a private showing for his friend and mentor Roberto Rossellini. Rossellini was quietly appreciative but not effusive. He later confessed he felt a mix of emotions; his mentee was now a filmmaker to be reckoned with. It was clear that Rossellini didn't know what to make of it.

The slight rebuff only made Federico more sure of himself. He was more insistent than ever to forge his own path. He had formed a team of colleagues with whom he wanted to continue to work: the writers Tullio Pinelli and Ennio Flaiano, composer Nino Rota, and director of photography Otello Martelli. Giulietta had turned in another stellar performance playing a character Federico had named Cabiria. The character stayed with him and he kept it in his mind for the future.

The White Sheik opened at the Venice Film Festival. It received mixed reviews; some were scathing and suggested that the director didn't possess the slightest aptitude for directing. But not everyone felt that way. The up-and-coming producers Carlo Ponti and Dino De Laurentiis took note. The criticism, if anything, spurred Federico onward. Giulietta, always a fierce defender of her husband, hated the negative reviews, although her own reviews always seemed to be positive.

"I hate the judgments, the pontificating," she said.

Federico replied, "In Emilia-Romagna when I was growing up with my grandmother in Gambettola, there was a saying, 'The man who has been laughed at goes arrogantly ahead.'"

Federico was poised to forge ahead. But he did so by revisiting parts of his past.

At the age of thirty-two, in 1952, Federico had now lived away from Rimini for almost twelve years. But the memories of his childhood and youth formed an indelible lens through which his dreams and artistry were shaped. The script for *I Vitelloni* came mainly from the people Federico had observed so carefully while growing up; in this case, a certain sect of young men who were in their early to mid-twenties when Federico was a teenager. The interlocking stories of five such young men from a provincial town formed the basis for the film. The word *vitelloni* means "young calves" and was an expression used to describe lazy young men in their twenties who lived off their parents when they were perfectly capable of supporting themselves. They were neither terribly poor nor terribly wealthy; they came from a class of Italian provincials who grew up postwar and had just enough to get by. They weren't terribly motivated by anything except sleeping, eating, having sexual conquests, and socializing with peers. They had no ambition but satisfying their urges and no particular thought about the future.

Lorenzo Pegoraro, an experienced producer, agreed to the

idea for a story about young men growing up in a provincial town. As the script progressed, the characters began to come into focus.

Fausto, the good-looking rake, is unfaithful to his pregnant bride. Alberto, the immature daydreamer, lives off the hard work and sacrifice of his mother and sister. Leopoldo, the intellectual, wants to be a playwright. Riccardo is a would-be singer. There is a sense throughout that these four characters would be content to remain in the provincial town for the rest of their lives. Moraldo, the fifth character, has the gift to imagine a life outside the strictures of the small town. He is both a part of the group and an observer.

The story follows the lives of all five characters, yet the broader scope of *I Vitelloni* explores what happens to a society that for decades has been crushed by the lack of choice and the repression of Fascism and its attempts to find its way among the ravages. The friends explore the town, attend parties and weddings, play billiards, roam the desolate streets at dawn; their home lives reveal a sense of desperation and stultification. In the end, Moraldo finds he must escape. He befriends a young boy—a part of the younger, possibly more hopeful, generation—and waves goodbye to his friends as he boards a train for Rome.

Federico had endless arguments with Lorenzo Pegoraro about casting. He insisted on casting Alberto Sordi in the key role of Alberto the daydreamer. Federico's own brother, Riccardo Fellini, in truth an aspiring singer, was cast as Riccardo the singer. Leopoldo Trieste, who had starred in *The White Sheik,* was Leopoldo the playwright. Franco Fabrizi was Fausto. Franco Interlenghi would play Moraldo.

Federico began his unusual casting methods while working on *I Vitelloni*. Actor Franco Interlenghi was asked to come to the casting office, and when he did so, he was ushered into a large room covered on all sides with red velvet curtains. He had the distinct notion he was being watched. He sat on a chair for a while. No one came. He left. He got the part and learned that Federico had indeed been hiding behind the curtains; he just wanted to watch how Interlenghi "behaved." He wanted to observe his face, his movements, capture his essence while he wasn't "acting." Apparently he passed the test.

Shooting began in Viterbo in December 1952. Pegoraro was so upset by the casting, and in particular that of Sordi, that he locked himself in the bathroom on the first day and refused to come out. Federico, on the other hand, was in his element. He knew the world, he knew the lives and motivations of his characters, and he approached the work with a confidence that helped elicit specific performances out of each of the actors. The gray rolling sea that draws the five friends toward the melancholy realization that their youth is quickly fading, that the uncertainty and responsibility of adulthood looms ahead, presents both a boundary and possibility. The relationships between the *vitelloni* as they lumber into the future are captured in all their complexity.

When Fellini finished the film, he and Pegoraro looked for a distributor. They began the long trek of taking the film around

Rome and hoping they could find someone interested enough to handle distribution. One tanned and coiffed fellow fell asleep twice during the showing. When he wasn't napping, he was on the phone or flirting with his secretaries. At the conclusion, his only question was about the make of the cars in the film. This encounter would be the first in a lifetime of Federico's tangles with the money men.

Pegoraro was so sure the film would be a disaster that he sold the rights. The cast gathered at the Grand Hotel des Bains at the Venice Film Festival and awaited the verdict. Like the *vitelloni* of the film, they enjoyed themselves immensely, and Federico, looking over the gathered crowd, savored the moment. It was a frenzied atmosphere. The film was an immediate hit with the audience, who responded with passion and enthusiasm. Recognizing their own lives in the five vagabonds, they applauded wildly.

I Vitelloni was a box office success. It won the Silver Lion award and sales outside Italy guaranteed Fellini's first widespread international recognition. Alberto Sordi soared to fame and made fourteen films in 1954 alone. Federico was besieged with offers to make sequels or other films about the characters. He was even offered the idea of doing a female version, *I Vitellini.* Federico turned them all down. He had zero interest in pursuing another film on the subject. Among all his talents as a screenwriter and filmmaker, perhaps it was this aspect of his artistic nature that was most admirable and prevalent: He insisted on telling the stories he wanted to tell from his own soul. He refused to create simply for the money.

Meanwhile, intellectual filmmaker Cesare Zavattini, a friend of Federico's, had contacted him just after he had finished editing *I Vitelloni*. Would Federico like to make a short film about love in the city of Rome? It would be part of a bill of short films with other respected filmmakers, among them Michelangelo Antonioni and Vittorio De Sica. The idea of working on something short and relatively simple appealed to Federico and he immediately came up with an idea. He touted the story as being true. It wasn't. But Zavattini believed him. It concerned a young woman who comes to a matrimonial agency desperate for marriage and agrees to marry a werewolf. The film echoed Federico's great love of Kafka. Coming out a month after the enduring success of *I Vitelloni,* it was further proof of the personal and unique vision of Federico Fellini.

I Vitelloni placed Federico in the center of Italy's most sought-after filmmakers. Yet he still lived with Giulietta and her Aunt Giulia in the apartment on via Lutezia.

"Perhaps we can consider moving," said Giulietta wistfully one day in early May of 1952.

"Perhaps someone will let me make the film I really want to make. I want to make a movie with you. You are my muse, my inspiration, the finest actress I know," answered Federico.

"If you could get Sophia Loren for the main role, you'd have producers in the palm of your hand," said Giulietta.

"You have something no one else has. You are unique. You are a clown. Clowns make people laugh. They also break hearts," answered Federico.

Giulietta took him in with her deep brown eyes. They were

full of pride, pain, and hope. "Do you really think the world is ready for a clown like me?"

"If I can show the world who you are, your heart, your soul, they will never stop wanting you."

Chapter Six

THE DREAM OF REDEMPTION

Federico and Giulietta took a vacation in the Alps to celebrate the success of *I Vitelloni.* They had never traveled together for pleasure. Their only previous trips had been for work. They drove the Fiat Topolino over the narrow mountain roads linking ancient villages that clung to the sides of the mountains. They saw whole villages that remained destroyed by the bombing during the war. They also saw reconstruction, which gave them hope. What fascinated Federico the most, however, were the small fairs and circuses they found in some of the small towns and villages. Some were large, with tents and animals, reminiscent of the circus in Rimini. Others consisted of only one or two specialty performers who motored from village to village, gathering a crowd, performing their feats and passing the hat. As Federico and Giulietta traveled the roads in their shiny Fiat, they came upon wizened performers slowly making their way from town to town, camping at night on the sides of the forlorn highways. Federico supposed there had been performers doing this since medieval times. Their mutual isolation and dependence touched him. The magic that they brought for a moment to the villages, despite their own limited circumstances, was seared into his memory.

When they returned from the vacation, Federico met with Tullio Pinelli, who had just come from visiting his extended family in Turin.

"I saw a couple struggling up the autostrade," Pinelli said. "A little cart with a mermaid banner on the side. Their tire had blown. This tiny leathery-skinned woman was pushing and this big brute of a man was pulling. They were some kind of gypsies or circus performers. The mermaid banner broke away and fluttered to the top of the tree at the side of the road. He shimmied up the tree and retrieved it and on they went. It was positively Sisyphean."

Federico, who believed strongly in omens, decided that this was their next film.

They began to write the script for *La Strada*. It would be the story of Zampano, a brutish circus strongman who takes on the sister of the woman who had been his previous assistant on the road. A simple woman, Gelsomina is sold by her mother to the strongman as a replacement for her sister, who is destitute. As they travel from village to village, she learns to perform and becomes a part of the act. She attempts to bring light and hope to their meager lives. She is treated cruelly by Zampano, but remains loyal to him.

One night Gelsomina wanders away from their camp and meets an acrobat. The acrobat, Il Mato, is a teacher and philosopher. Il Mato offers her understanding and empathy. He teaches her to play the trumpet—a haunting tune that would be composed by Nino Rota for the film. Il Mato also relentlessly teases Zampano and brings him to a murderous rage. When Zampano is jailed, Gelsomina has a chance to escape. She decides to remain with Zampano. When Gelsomina and Zampano come upon Il Mato on a deserted road, Zampano kills him. Gelsomina cannot reconcile this final act of brutality. Zampano leaves her, isolated on a lonely road. Years later, a guilt-ravaged Zampano hears someone whistling the mournful tune and finds Gelsomina lived and died there. The final scene of the film shows Zampano prostrate on the sand at the edge of the sea, looking to the heavens for redemption.

The script they wrote was pronounced by Ennio Flaiano to be too mystical and not grounded enough in reality. This was the role Flaiano always played within the triumvirate of Federico, Tullio Pinelli, and himself. The final script reflected an even more gritty narrative, with the couple coming into a town and Zampano leaving her for another woman. Gelsomina is left by the side of the road for the entire night. In the morning, a riderless horse clops by as Gelsomina crouches on the curb.

With the script completed, Federico began to make the rounds of producers. Most rejected the project outright. They continued to beg him to do a sequel to *I Vitelloni.* They were interested in Federico but not in *La Strada.* They completely rejected the notion that Giulietta should play the lead in a film and made suggestions for stars who could guarantee box office success. Burt Lancaster and Sylvia Mangano, the glamorous wife of Dino De Laurentiis, were two ideas they put forth. Federico rejected them. Luigi Pegoraro, another potential producer, refused to see Giulietta as anything but the prostitute in *Without Pity*.

Finally the producing team of Dino De Laurentiis and Carlo Ponti signed on to *La Strada*. They still didn't like the property, but they hoped that they could have future work with Federico. The two men had divergent personalities and ideas about the film business. De Laurentiis was steeped in the factory notion of Hollywood filmmaking and was focused on cranking out films with an eye to quantity over quality. Ponti was more discerning. They both respected the potential of the thirty-three-year-old Fellini, but were highly skeptical of *La Strada*. They hired Gigetto Giacosi, a tough and unrelenting production manager, to supervise the production. He would have his hands full.

De Laurentiis and Ponti kept up a campaign to convince Federico to cast a beautiful starlet in the role of Gelsomina, but he was adamant about Giulietta. She had a small role in a film that was shooting at Cinecittà and, ever vigilant about his wife's work, Federico went to visit the set. It was a film called *Angels of Darkness* and starred Anthony Quinn and Richard Basehart, two American actors.

Quinn was part of a late 1940s and early 1950s diaspora of young talent from Hollywood. Victims of the Hollywood studio system that pigeonholed them into restricted roles and long contracts, Quinn, Basehart, Kirk Douglas, Burt Lancaster, Farley Granger, and many others came to work in Rome. Quinn was a Mexican-American actor who had made many films under the studio system, usually playing generic ethnic tough guys. He took a break from Hollywood and replaced Marlon Brando on Broadway in the original production of *A Streetcar Named Desire*. He was a serious actor and visual artist who had studied to become an architect. He returned to Hollywood and gained elevated status when he won an Academy Award for Best Supporting Actor in Elia Kazan's *Viva Zapata*. Despite his success, he was disillusioned with the strictures of Hollywood.

The moment Federico saw Anthony Quinn on the set of *Angels of Darkness* that day, he knew he had found his Zampano. The actor exuded the brutal force and earthiness the character demanded. Federico pursued him for days, going to the set and explaining the story to Quinn over and over. Quinn had never heard of Fellini and had no interest.

Ingrid Bergman broke the logjam, inviting the two men to dinner and screening *I Vitelloni*. Quinn was dumbfounded by what he considered a masterpiece. He immediately agreed to do *La Strada*. Federico also cast Richard Basehart, from the cast of *Angels of Darkness,* as Il Mato. In Basehart's handsome face, kindly manner, and physical agility, Federico knew he had found his gentle clown.

With the script complete, the casting process finished, and the producing team in place, Federico gave the screenplay to Giulietta to read. It was just after the summer holidays, 1953, and *La Strada* was set to begin shooting in October. He paced the floor of their bedroom on via Lutezia as she lay prone on her stomach on their bed, taking it all in. When she finished, the pages were wet with her tears. She reached up and hugged Federico, kissing his face, making it wet with tears, too.

"It is so beautiful. So sad. Gelsomina is you, Federico, traveling on the road of life, enduring so many things, and always, always so full of wonder and hope. Hope. Always hope."

Federico shed a tear or two himself. He valued the opinion of his wife.

Giulietta went on. "She is like a Cinderella. Light. Transforming from beginning to end like a butterfly. I see her beginning as a little tramp-like figure and emerging at the end as a beautiful woman." Giulietta sat down at her dressing table and surveyed herself in the mirror. She began to arrange her hair in an attractive manner.

Federico bent down and looked at his wife in the mirror. He was frowning.

"I don't see her that way at all. She is simple-minded, almost deficient mentally. She remains plain, quirky, almost ugly, like an artichoke, throughout. She dresses in rags and is bedraggled from beginning to end. The beauty of her soul shines through."

He took a glob of face cream and massaged it into her hair. He flicked talcum powder on her face. He took rouge and put a red circle on the end of her nose. He grabbed a black pencil and drew two quizzical eyebrows. The whole effect was that of a Kabuki-like clown with a mop of greasy hair.

Giulietta began to cry. Her tears streaked the white makeup. They were tears of anger this time.

"I won't go in front of a camera looking like this, do you hear me?"

Federico was equally insistent that she would. Or else. "I have fought every producer in Hollywood to insist on you. But

I could go with Sylvia Mangano. Or Sophia Loren. They would die to do this role."

"They'd kill themselves before they would allow themselves to be photographed like this."

"To me, this is Gelsomina!" yelled Federico.

"To ME, this is humiliation!" screamed Giulietta.

Auntie Giulia heard the row and quietly closed her bedroom door. She turned on the radio. She had heard their arguments before. This one lasted for hours.

Three weeks later, *La Strada* began shooting at the Sisters of Clare Convent in Bagnoregio. Giulietta looked exactly as she had the night of the argument. Added to her appearance was bleached blond hair that had been cut by Federico the way he remembered his grandmother in Gamboletta had done it, with an overturned bowl. Her wardrobe had been found in the bins of the flea market at Porta Portese in Rome. The final feature was an actual shepherd's cape made of scratchy moth-eaten fur.

Giulietta had accepted Federico's vision and, as she was a great actress, had developed a whole physicality for the character. Gelsomina had stooped shoulders from the physical labor, but feet that were loose and could move and dance. She learned to convey a world of emotion with her face.

The shoot, which took place in remote locations in Bagnoregio, Ovindoli, Roccaraso, and Viterbo, was low budget. Cast and crew often found themselves, after exhausting days, in hotels without heat or hot water. Anthony Quinn, used to the luxury of his own trailer and three personal assistants, was shocked to find his dressing room a stool with a shard of mirror stuck to a wall, and having to do his own makeup. Nonetheless, Quinn, who was also an artist and architect, began to appreciate the artistry that Federico brought to his work.

The deep commitment Federico drew from everyone was impressive. The performances he was drawing out of Giulietta and Basehart were astounding. His perfectionism and attention to detail were clear; he looked at over fifty cigarette boxes one day before he chose the right one for Zampano.

Extras from family circuses such as the Zamperla lent authenticity to the encounters with the performers. Sevitri, a strongman and clown, was brought to the set to instruct Quinn, who absorbed every lesson. Federico was in his element. The humanity and mystery, the human search for connection, and the isolation of being alive on the road of life were poured into Federico's work on the film.

As directors and other artists from around the world began to hear about *La Strada,* they visited the set. Federico welcomed them. Unlike many directors, he loved visitors and onlookers to his sets; he felt they brought energy and life. Elia Kazan was shocked to find an atmosphere more like a real circus, complete with hawkers of food and music. His sets, and those of many Hollywood directors, were quiet, calm, and absolutely focused. Federico's were full of constant noise, chatter, and seeming disorder. Because he dubbed the lines after shooting, he spoke constantly to the actors while shooting a scene: "Look over there. Like you have lost someone dear. More slowly. You are about to jump off a cliff. Yes, yes. Crying but not crying. Brilliant. No. Turn. A little more slowly. Now snap back over to the right. He has broken your heart and you can't let him know . . ." and so forth. It was Federico's method of getting exactly what he wanted. The outer chaos on the set was something that fed him. But there was nothing chaotic about his vision of the film. He knew precisely what he wanted and pursued it with a mathematical precision.

Other visitors included Father Angelo Arpa, a Catholic priest and cinephile who was a friend of Federico's. He would prove to be a liaison between Federico and church censors. Brunello Rondi was another friend who often visited the set. He was a prolific writer and screenwriter who became a collaborator and trusted advisor to his friend Federico. The director was always happy to consider opinions. But in the end, he always did what he felt served the film.

Giulietta sprained her ankle in mid-January, setting the shoot back three weeks. Quinn, who was contracted to start shooting *Attila,* also for De Laurentiis, had to work on both sets each day. His haggard appearance and exhaustion lent gravitas to his performance of Zampano. The film went over budget and De Laurentiis bargained with Federico to pay him back by agreeing to direct some pickup shots for *Attila.* Federico gladly obliged.

In late April, after months of exhausting work, Giulietta began to notice a change in Federico. He became listless and depressed. Worried about her husband and unsure of whether he would be able to complete the project when it was so near the finish line, she insisted that he see a therapist. For a short time, Federico became a patient of the psychoanalyst Emilio Servadio, a former musician and lawyer with diverse interests in psychology, hypnosis, and parapsychology. As one of the founders of the Italian Psychoanalytic Society, Servadio encouraged Federico to excavate his childhood memories, fears, and traumas. Federico was only able to agree to several sessions. Then his distaste for sitting in one place, immobile, and talking about himself overcame him.

After his fourth appointment, Federico felt he had had enough. He left Servadio's office hurriedly in the middle of a Roman thunderstorm. He ran out of the building, feeling a flood of fear as he realized the weight of finishing *La Strada*. The actors and crew were depending on him. The producers had spent their money and they wanted their product. The rain was blowing in his face. There was only one person standing on the street. It was a woman carrying a large umbrella. She beckoned Federico to come and stand underneath the shelter. She was a tall, attractively dressed woman. She was dressed elegantly. Her name was Lia. She was not an artist and had nothing to do with the world of film. She had no idea who Federico was.

For the next several years Federico saw her secretly. They had a relationship separate from the demands of his public life. She asked nothing of him except occasional companionship. No one knew about her except Federico's childhood friend, Titta.

On the night of September 6, 1954, *La Strada* was screened at the Venice Film Festival. Federico had indeed been able to finish the film, but because of the delays, the snow, which was to be a part of the final scenes, had disappeared. It had to be created out of bags of plaster and linen sheets borrowed from people in the nearby town. Giulietta and Federico came to

Venice under a cloud of headlines that claimed she was having an affair with Richard Basehart. Federico couldn't tell if it was true. Their relationship had undergone changes. He had been unfaithful to Giulietta as a husband. But not as an artist. That was still clear. They supported one another as artists. Federico was Giulietta's inspiration. Giulietta was Federico's breath of life. They clung to one another as they entered the theater.

They were surrounded by every important director, actor, and critic who was anyone in Italian cinema. *La Strada* was shown in an atmosphere of political strife between Communists and Christian Democrats. It was hard, if not impossible, to judge the film on its own merits. There were groups in the audience who vociferously supported the elegant director Vittorio De Sica and others equally passionate who supported young upstart filmmakers like Fellini. When *La Strada* was not given first prize, despite its obvious brilliance, and De Sica's film was also passed over, a fistfight broke out between Moraldo Rossi, a supporter of Fellini, and Franco Zeffirelli, who was an ardent De Sica fan. As Federico and Giulietta hurried away and exited the theater, they were greeted by a rapturous ovation from the crowds outside.

Although *La Strada* did not win high acclaim in Italy, the reviews and responses internationally were uniformly positive, heralding the film as a breakthrough in the language of cinema. By the time it was nominated for an Academy Award for Best Foreign Language film in 1957, it had garnered over fifty different awards and prizes. Federico and Giulietta joined Tullio Pinelli and Dino De Laurentiis in attending the awards ceremony at the Pantages Theatre in Hollywood on March 27, 1957. As Federico watched De Laurentiis accept the award for *La Strada,* his first thought was that he would now get financing for his next film. He didn't feel his own English was strong enough to make a speech if he won. He found America confusing and tiresome. The over-orchestrated and overproduced American version of Rota's simple melody for Gelsomina, which in America was recorded as a song called "Stars Shine in Your Eyes," was a perfect example of a culture he couldn't comprehend.

Federico and Giulietta spent nine days in America after receiving the Academy Award. Their days were filled with publicity stunts and endless offers to make films in America. Several television talk shows booked Federico for interviews and his American publicist insisted he agree to go. When he understood that they wanted him to make spaghetti on-air and demonstrate how to kiss a woman's hand, Federico flatly refused. He was offered $250,000, an unheard-of sum, to direct a western. He gently but firmly turned down the offer. Burt Lancaster, who had his own production company, invited Federico to a meeting. His company wanted to discuss a sequel to the Gelsomina story: *The Adventures of Gelsomina.* Federico pretended to consider the offer out of politeness. The last thing he wanted to do was to offend these people who seemed to have money by the truckload. The American market was a vital and essential one, and he had no desire to do anything that would diminish interest in or sales of his films in America. On the other hand, he was done with Gelsomina. He had said all he wanted to say about her.

Federico found himself wanting only to return to Rome and to work. Although he resisted saying it out loud, he knew that making a film in America would be impossible for him. How could he know the thoughts of a Midwestern housewife? The speech patterns of a taxi driver in Manhattan? What was in the lunchbox of a day laborer in Chicago? He found the culture in America fascinating but impenetrable. The vastness of Los Angeles was nearly incomprehensible; the amusement park Disneyland, which he visited, was a bizarre landscape. The money available in Hollywood seemed endless. But what exactly did it all add up to? Federico supposed the award might mitigate the disaster caused by the film he had insisted on making after *La Strada*: *Il Bidone*.

He had wanted to make another film about the way in which innocents are abused, this time from the point of view of the abusers. Federico reflected on *Il Bidone* on the long plane ride back to Rome. He had been besieged, as usual, to make some sort of sequel to *La Strada*. Instead he had made a film about swindlers.

Based on his fascination for the underworld of people who cheat and steal, *Il Bidone* had been an examination of the actions and mindsets of people who steal and cheat others for a living. Federico had been struck, when he first moved to Rome, by meeting a man named Lupaccio, literally called "the wolf" because of his reputation for cheating and lying. He worked for Lupaccio for a very short time trying to pawn off fake diamonds for the real thing. Federico was ultimately repulsed by the notion.

He quit his job for Lupaccio after one distasteful experience. But he remained interested in the psychology of people who lie for a living.

His own father spent half a lifetime lying to his mother. People had survived during and after the war by lying and cheating. The black market fed and clothed thousands. Who could blame them? They had to feed and clothe their loved ones. Federico himself was married and now had a secret relationship unknown to Giulietta. He thought about the rumors that Giulietta had a relationship with Richard Basehart. *They are friends,* acknowledged Federico, looking out at the clouds as the plane banked, *but are they more than that?*

He thought about the actor Broderick Crawford, whose visage Federico had seen on a torn movie poster in Piazza del Popolo. He had insisted in hiring Crawford, not knowing that he was a recovering alcoholic. Who could have known that the wine festival in San Marino would be happening and that Crawford would return to his drunken, alcoholic ways? He had been drunk every day. Federico encouraged laughter, life, fun on his sets. But there was an internal discipline normally brought by actors who had come from live theater—Giulietta's iron-clad focus, for example. This was something nearly every actor he had worked with had possessed. For Federico, it was a given. Not for Crawford. They had to tie ropes to his feet and shoulders some days to get him to move. They had to post his lines on microphone stands and in trees. And yet, that craggy face expressed both the venality and the vulnerability of Augusto with depth and naturalism. There were times when Federico had been exasperated with his drunkenness. And then times when his misery and pain were seared into the camera. The final scene, in which Augusto, full of remorse, dies with his face crushed into the rocky side of a mountain still moved Federico.

It was the wrong film for a country becoming giddy with its own upbeat economy. Italian society did not want to think about swindlers and liars and remorse. The Catholic Church was offended by the portrayal of swindlers who dressed like priests. *It was treated vilely in Venice,* remembered Federico, *so much so that it seemed they were delighted in tearing me limb from limb. I will never go back to the Venice Film Festival.*

Federico looked at this wife, dozing in the airplane seat next to him. Her makeup was perfect; her hair had been coiffed into a blond cloud; she wore a Pucci dress. It was a far cry from Gelsomina. She was now a world-renowned actress, internationally known and respected. She received fan letters from women around the globe. They were often heartbreaking descriptions of abuse and betrayal. There were Gelsomina clubs in all the major cities of Italy. Disney wanted to make Gelsomina dolls and suggested an animated Gelsomina cartoon. *All this came from you, Giulietta. What I saw in you,* thought Federico. *Gelsomina is our daughter,* La Strada *the road leading to our purpose in life.*

The plane began to descend toward Rome. Federico could see the blue waves of the sea. The Dome of St. Peter's came into view and it gave him great comfort. They landed and made their way to via Archimede in the Parioli neighborhood. They had lived in the apartment for over a year. They had moved, finally, from the cozy apartment on via Lutezia with Auntie Giulia and so many memories. The dear lady had passed away not long after.

Stunned and saddened by the death of someone so dear, Federico had gone for a visit to Rimini to see his father. Federico was shocked by how old Urbano looked. They had gone to dinner and Federico hoped it would be an intimate evening between father and son. But Urbano was not so old that he couldn't invite an attractive woman they met at the bar of the Grand Hotel to join them for dinner. The heartfelt evening between father and son never happened. Urbano passed away on May 1, 1956. Federico went home for the funeral and stayed in Rimini for several weeks, visiting Titta Benzi and other old friends.

When he arrived home at 114 via Archimede on May 31, 1956, he stepped outside to his terrace to look at his beloved Rome. He saw an odd sight. A helicopter was delivering a large statue of Christ to the Vatican. It hung by a long rope as the chopper made its way across the city with its precious cargo. On a nearby terrace, bikini-clad women waved and cheered. The helicopter pilot saluted the beauties and flew on to his papal destination. Federico, who believed fervently in signs and omens, felt it was a kind of benediction. He kept this image, as he did all he saw, in his memory bank.

Federico sighed with relief, abandoning his thoughts and musings for the moment, as the plane from Los Angeles descended toward Rome. The city of Rome had become his creative home and during his sojourn in Los Angeles, he had missed the inspiration he found there. As the taxi made its way down via Archimede, Federico remembered that he and Giulietta had yet to fully furnish their own home even though they had been there for over a year. It seemed they never had the time.

Their maid had lit a fire in the outdoor fireplace on the terrace. It overlooked the Villa Elia, with its golden walls and manicured gardens. Giulietta sat on one of the large blue armchairs on the terrace. She was curled in its depths with her eyes closed.

Federico was exhausted but restless. He got up and looked over the edge of the balustrade at the street below, with its gleaming brass doorknobs and clipped hedges. It was a far cry from L'acquedotto Felice, in northern Rome. Federico had explored the neighborhood and the seamy side of Roman nightlife for an entire year after making *Il Bidone.* Pier Pasolini, a brilliant young filmmaker and ardent supporter, had led Federico on a yearlong nightly journey while researching the film *Nights of Cabiria,* through the streets filled with prostitutes and nightclubs that catered to every appetite.

The film had been inspired by a streetwalker named Wanda. Federico had discovered her living in a shack near a location shoot for *Il Bidone.* She was initially outraged that Federico had encroached on her "home," a shack made of discarded railroad siding. But gradually, bringing her lunches from the set, Federico befriended her. She inspired his next film. Dino De Laurentiis did not want to produce a film about a prostitute. He handed the project over to his intellectual brother, Luigi, who was thrilled to work with Fellini. Piero Gherardi, the costume and set designer, and Pier Pasolini opened Federico's eyes to a whole new side of Rome. By day, Federico had made the rounds of potential producers, actors, and crew, many of whom were aghast at the notion of financing or working on a film about Roman streetwalkers. By night Federico had scoured the underworld of Rome. Giulietta had been filled with concern when he had come home as the sun was rising.

Giulietta was, however, excited to land the role of Cabiria, the lead. Shooting began July 6, 1956. It was grueling and difficult, and her working relationship with Federico had been combative. Giulietta complained that he was hardest on her—exacting and unrelenting. She asked for costumes that would be flattering. She got thrift shop finds once again, this time put together by Piero Gherardi. Gherardi did exquisite work on the film with detailed attention to costumes, sets, and set dressing. Nino Rota wrote the score for *Nights of Cabiria* while watching rushes of the film as he sat at a piano. Otello Martelli, the famed director of photography, also worked on the film. With *Nights of Cabiria,* Federico had solidified the extraordinary group of collaborators that would continue to work with him for years.

Federico insisted on including a "man with a sack" episode that detailed a lone man who went around to the poor and disenfranchised delivering food and succor. He was not affiliated with the Church or any organized religion. When it came time for a representative from the Catholic Church to see the film with regard to censorship, Federico and Gherardi put together a special screening room complete with a purple throne. The screening room was located in a questionable neighborhood, and as the entourage watched the film inside, Federico and his producers stood outside, being solicited by the denizens of the area. The Church gave its approval with the exception of the "man with the sack" scene. He was offensive because he was not an official of the Catholic Church.

One evening, Federico smiled as he beheld his sleeping wife. *Nights of Cabiria* would premiere in several months. Until then, and the next spate of opinions and reviews, they could rest, for a moment, on the award they were given in America. It would go in the room they had designated the "award room." It was an empty bedroom in their new penthouse apartment that would house the growing mass of international acclaim: statues, statuettes, citations, and plaques the two artists began to gather. They were appreciated—a sign of public acclaim. But to both artists they only paved the way for the possibility of the next project.

It was now black-velvet midnight in the sky above Rome. Giulietta stirred and Federico covered her with another blanket. She had been outraged by his endless nights exploring the city's underworld with Pasolini and Gherardi. She hated Pasolini in particular and thought he was a bad influence. *Perhaps so,* thought Federico, *but the role I created for you, Cabiria, is the greatest gift I could give you.* Federico sat in the chair next to his wife and looked up at the Roman sky.

He awoke with a start. He was still sitting next to Giulietta. The dawn was breaking and Giulietta was still asleep. She could sleep anywhere, anytime. *Her conscience is clear,* Federico reasoned. The world would soon see her Cabiria. They would soon love her even more than they already did, although Federico wondered how that would even be possible. He laughed as he realized they now had a big, wide bed with Pratesi linens. They had a maid to turn down their silk comforter. And they still slept out on the terrace. *We are essentially two vagabonds, two gypsies, two dreamers,* he thought.

The light came up over St. Peter's. Federico watched as the sun lit its dome. Giulietta's hand slipped away from her blanket. Federico reached for it. It was cold. Her fingers intertwined with his and squeezed until his wedding ring dug into the bones of his hands. It hurt. But they stayed that way until the sun came up.

Chapter Seven

THE DREAM OF THE PRESENT

Federico had just taken his last sip of a late-night espresso. It was 1:00 a.m. on a steamy August night in 1958. The raucous crowd at the Café de Paris was beginning to thin out. He was just about to lay his tiny gold-rimmed cup into the saucer when the table was overturned by his companions, a group of young photographers, who sprang into action with lightning speed. With a crash of silver and glassware they surrounded their prey like a pack of hyenas. Some held flashbulbs and others snapped away with rat-a-tat precision. The evening on via Veneto had until then been a relatively quiet one. Now it exploded to life.

King Farouk, the object of the photographers, had lost his Egyptian throne nearly a decade earlier. He had taken up residence in Rome and become a denizen of the caffès on via Veneto. Constantly surrounded by a menacing entourage of Albanian bodyguards and fashionable women he paid to keep him company, the ex-king was known to eat three meals in an evening. His three-hundred-pound body was topped by a small head with squinty eyes that peered out at the world behind owl-like glasses. Having lost his kingdom in Egypt, he held court in Rome on the via Veneto, hosting celebrities and royalty from around the world at his tables. The public had become used to his visage, so photos of King Farouk at ease were no longer newsworthy. Pictures of him in a froth or attacking photographers sold like hotcakes, however. An angry Farouk caught in the act of physically assaulting photographers was worth anything it took to provoke the rotund ex-king.

Federico observed the entire event with fascination. He had been keeping company with the pack of photographers for weeks now. They were charmed by his interest. They had let him into their late-night fraternity. Tazio Secchiaroli and Pierluigi Praturlon were not only pugnacious—they were also skilled photographers. They had been adolescents during the postwar years when GIs and tourists were happy to pay them for photographs in front of Rome's famous monuments. The tourists would pay up front and then be given an address where they could pick up the developed photos the following day. It was a business that allowed the young photographers to support themselves and their starving families in the lean years after the war. It was a business ruined by the invention of the Brownie camera. When individual tourists had their own cameras, they had no need for photographers.

The burgeoning Italian film industry during the 1950s and the intersection of Hollywood producers and stars saved these photographers and gave them a new livelihood. As Hollywood filmmakers began to recognize the financial advantages of working in Rome combined with the skilled technicians available at Cinecittà and other studios, they began to flock to the city. Films like *Ben-Hur* and *Roman Holiday* displayed Rome's history and charm to international audiences. In addition, Americans working in Rome enjoyed the first $20,000 they made there tax-free. Rome began to be known as "Hollywood on the Tiber" as major American productions made films in Rome that were international box office successes.

The Italian fashion industry began to boom, with designers like Pucci and Brioni who proved that design, luxurious fabrics, and unique tailoring could attract international markets and compete successfully with the Parisian stronghold. Stars such as Sophia Loren, Ava Gardner, and Elizabeth Taylor were photographed wearing these creations. The images excited fans and created Italian fashion empires.

Via Veneto in the late 1950s had become the place where all of these erstwhile celebrities gathered. Movie producers came to make deals. Stars came to be seen. Entourages swirled around the rich and famous. Tourists came to gape at the whole scene.

Via Vittorio Veneto was a boulevard that began its meander from the Piazza Barberini and ran uphill toward the Porta Pinciana. In ancient times, it was said that the area belonged to Messalina, the wife of Emperor Claudius, and that it was her playground for debauchery. More recently, in the seventeenth century, it was a part of the Villa Ludovisi and was owned by a cardinal. Its gardens and spectacular views were enjoyed by visiting nobility. In the nineteenth century, as a part of Risorgimento, it was divided into parcels. Vittorio via Veneto, the street Romans shortened to Via Veneto, was named after the Battle of Vittorio Veneto, a decisive Italian victory of World War I. Horse chestnut trees were planted up and down the sides of the winding street. The inclusion of the Hotel Excelsior at one end, with its cupolas and five-star accommodations, began to attract a crowd that demanded luxury.

Other expensive hotels sprang up around the Excelsior. Caffès, bookshops, and bars followed. The upper end of the street reminded some of Paris. The lower end of the street, with its twists and turns and inviting trattorias, was distinctly Roman. The part of via Veneto near Piazza Barberini was also home to the Santa Maria della Concezione dei Cappuccini, an ancient monastery where the bones of monks were on display to remind viewers of the mortality that awaits all living human beings and, perhaps, to consider living a moral life.

The exhortations to be found at the monastery seemed to have little effect on the revelers who populated via Veneto in the late 1950s. The awakening of postwar Italy to the modern world, with its forays into fashion, cinema, and manufacturing, and the economic boom that followed, coincided with the death of Pope Pius XII and the ascendance of Pope John XXIII, who sought to embrace the modern world while still adhering to tradition. Curfews loosened, Romans celebrated, and nightlife in Rome exploded. Via Veneto became a stage set for celebrity, for indulgences of all kinds—a place to be seen, to drink, dance, flirt, and flaunt every excess.

None of it, however, was meaningful to the glittery celebrity crowds unless it was advertised and gobbled up by the public. Photographers became profoundly aware of this in the early

1950s when a case involving a young woman found dead on a beach near Rome scandalized the city, particularly when the crime was attached to a nearby mansion and a party attended by well-known politicians and wealthy industrialists. Although no one was ever convicted, the photographs of the accused and the family of Wilma Montesi, the victim, were seared into the public consciousness.

At the same time, Hollywood stars like Linda Christian and Tyrone Power, who were married in Rome dressed in fashions made by Italian designers, created a sensation when photographed. Sales of the designs were off the charts. Sales of the magazines in which the photographs appeared soared. The affair between the two married celebrities Ingrid Bergman and Roberto Rossellini provided endless fodder for gossip magazines and newspapers. The invention of the SLR zoom lens allowed photographers to take pictures from great distances, zeroing in on stars who were sunbathing on yachts, eating in restaurants, and cavorting in swimming pools.

People who had been starving for food and shelter during the war years now turned their attention to the lives of glamorous people who seemed to live above any moral laws of the universe. The constant churn of pictures that depicted lives dedicated to fashion, soirées, and decadence both fed and created more fascination on the part of the public. Photographers began to discover that if a still photo or a posed shot could be sold for a certain amount of money, the ones that really paid were the surprise shots catching a star unaware or off guard. If the star was "caught" in an unexpected moment of anger or debauchery, or out of control, all the better. If a still photo earned a photographer the equivalent of $40, one in which a star was livid might fetch $2,700. Photographers began to work together to create these moments. They swarmed unsuspecting celebrities, hid away in bushes and behind pillars, and shared information about where their prey might be, stalking them to catch them at their most vulnerable.

Federico had become friends with these photographers. They were potent symbols of the floating world of the unmoored, increasingly disconnected modern society in which he found himself. He was fascinated and repelled by it. One of the photographers was Tazio Secchiaroli, who had managed to document a scandalous evening in which a dancer stripped to the buff in the middle of a Roman street. He took pictures not only of the dancer herself, but of the surrounding crowd, the observers of the event. Pierluigi Praturlon also stood out as a photographer with consummate skill, confidence, and nerves of steel. He would stop at nothing to get his shot. Celebrities both befriended and feared him.

One of Praturlon's celebrity friends was Anita Ekberg, a Swedish actress and former Miss Sweden who had been working in Hollywood and who had become known for her pinups, gossip, and raucous personal life. In Rome to shoot a film, she and Praturlon had spent a night on the town dancing and drinking. Ekberg was known for her penchant to dance barefoot and had cut her foot. Staggering home, they happened on the Trevi Fountain. Ekberg insisted on bathing her foot in the waters of the fountain. Praturlon photographed her. The photo was an international sensation. When Federico saw the photograph, the idea for his next film crystalized: the sex goddess, the via Veneto, the rampaging photographers, a whole society poised on a cloud of moral turpitude, and a journalist, once an idealist and now jaded, in the center of it all.

Federico began to work on the script with an enthusiastic Ennio Flaiano, who was eager to write something that hearkened not to the past, as *La Strada* and *Nights of Cabiria* had done, but examined the present. Flaiano himself was a frequenter of the Café de Paris, the Rosati, the Strega-Zeppa, and the Doney, all favorite haunts of Rome's celebrity crowd. The idea of a journalist who is both attracted to and repulsed by the society in which he finds himself resonated with Federico's own state of international celebrity and the exhaustion of the constant spotlight. But the awards and the resulting fame allowed Federico to attract producers so that he could continue to make films.

Flaiano proposed a name for the photographer friend of the main character: Paparazzo. Federico liked the name because it sounded like buzzing insects—a perfect metaphor for the swarming hives of photographers. When filming began, the crew started calling them by the plural *paparazzi,* and the word became known and used worldwide.

Federico had a contract to direct the film with De Laurentiis producing. De Laurentiis despised the script. He gave it to three trusted friends whose opinion he respected. They felt the same way. They took particular distaste to the sequence in which a character who is an intellectual and a close friend of the main character kills his children and commits suicide. After a three-hour argument between De Laurentiis and Federico that could be heard throughout the entire office building in which it took place, De Laurentiis refused to produce the film as it was written. Federico had to find another producer who would make *La Dolce Vita* ("The Sweet Life"), as it had come to be called, the way that the writers envisioned. For Federico, the title was always one that was rife with irony.

"I am still obsessed with how hard it is for us to communicate with one another as human beings, one person to another," he said one night in November, 1958.

He was speaking to his friend Peppino Amato, a wealthy man and owner of several hotels, one of which was the Excelsior on via Veneto. Federico was on one of his many journeys around Rome to find new producers for *La Dolce Vita*. Tazio Secchiaroli had joined them, showing photos he had taken that very evening of a strip tease done by a woman on a street in Trastevere.

"Anita Ekberg challenged the woman, a belly dancer, to do it. The bongo drums started, and before you know it, a crowd had gathered. And there she was, naked as the day she was born, in the middle of a Roman street," said Secchiaroli.

Federico was most interested in the way in which the photos captured not only the shapely dancer, but also the crowd of amused and astonished onlookers. This was Secciaroli's specialty. The photos created a firestorm of public fascination, condemnation, and further fame for the paparazzi.

Amato called Federico the following day. "I'm in," he said, "if you are setting it on via Veneto. It will be good for business.

And call Angelo Rizzoli. He is a publisher but one of the wealthiest men in Italy. He wants to get into film."

Amato was correct. The meeting between Federico and Rizzoli began a relationship that was to last for more than a decade. The esteemed gentleman who had built an empire in publishing agreed to a contract to produce *La Dolce Vita* in October 1958. He bought out the contract from Dino De Laurentiis and created a company, Cineriz, to make the film. He initially treated Federico as if he were a kindly uncle to a brilliant, if slightly wayward, nephew.

Amato was included as one of the producers and proved to be pugnacious as well as excitable. At one meeting he grew so upset he claimed he would eat the script if certain changes weren't made. Federico refused. Amato began chewing the paper. At another meeting, Amato threatened to drink ink rather than sign for an increased budget. When Federico insisted on the increased budget, Amato drank the ink, much of which spilled down the front of his white shirt. A third time, Amato objected to the suicide scene and said he would drop his pants if the script were not altered. Federico let Amato know there would be no script changes. Amato disrobed. Federico enjoyed all of these scenes immensely. They gave him a kind of perverse admiration for the colorful producer.

On October 10, 1958, Pope Pius XII died. His death marked the end of an era in Rome. His papacy had seen the city through World War II and the postwar years, a time of unprecedented growth and change. He was virulently anti-Communist and schisms between the Communist Party and the Christian Democrats would continue to widen in the coming years. Pope John XXIII, his successor, would prove to be one of the most popular popes in modern times. His openness to change, evidenced by his convening of the Second Vatican Council, demonstrated his desire to reexamine old doctrines and disciplines. He traveled all around Rome and made himself known to the population; his roly-poly figure was beloved and his connection to young and old made him much revered. At the turn of the decade, Americans were about to elect the first Catholic president, the handsome, worldly John Fitzgerald Kennedy, who was married to the equally elegant Jacqueline Bouvier. The world seemed poised on a new frontier.

In the fall of 1959, Federico was deeply entrenched in preparations for *La Dolce Vita*. Hovering on the brink of a new decade, the now internationally known director was nearly forty years old. His nightly drives through Rome became his office hours. He variously took Dominique Delouche, a French critic who had become part of Federico's entourage; Piero Gherardi to discuss the look of the film; his co-writer Ennio Flaiano; or Pier Pasolini, the young writer and filmmaker Federico respected as the voice of youth. Both attracted to and repulsed by the decadence on via Veneto, they sought to tell the truth about a certain strata of Roman society at the turn of the decade.

Angelo Rizzoli, the paternalistic producer, suggested Paul Newman as the lead. Federico rejected this idea outright. He continued to cull through the stacks of photos and headshots he kept on his desk. They piled up on tables around the office and leaned in ever-increasing towers against the walls of the office. Federico went through them as he made and received phone calls in a never-ending stream; he considered offers and listened to pitches.

"I need someone nonspecific. A regular face. A face that could be every face. A face that doesn't call attention to itself," he told Giulietta one day. They were staying at the beach in Fregene, not far from Rome.

"Marcello Mastroianni," she said, bending the brim of her sunhat. "I've known him since my university theater days. He's been mired in milquetoast husband roles for years. But you'll like him. He's just the right combination of handsome face but laconic. He never tries too hard. But in the best way. What can I say? He's easy."

Federico called him immediately, and the next day Mastroianni arrived on the beach at Fregene. He brought his lawyer to make himself look more professional. Federico was sunning himself on the beach and he saw Mastroianni ambling toward him as if he were in no hurry to get there.

Federico squinted into the sun and, with no preamble, said, "Rizzoli wants me to hire Paul Newman, but I'd like to hire you."

Mastroianni looked out at the beach. It was a hot day. He took in three bathing beauties who were lying on their stomachs. He took in the full view of their backsides and said, indicating the sunbathers: "My day is already beautiful."

Federico nodded his agreement.

Mastroianni wasted no time getting down to business. "Do you suppose I could see a script?" He wanted to make some attempt at not looking too eager.

"Of course," said Federico, waving at Flaiano, who was also nearby.

Flaiano brought Mastroianni an envelope. It was thin and held only one sheet of paper. On it was one of Federico's sketches. It was of a man-dog paddling on the sea with a long penis that reached the ocean floor. Mermaids flew around his head in a circle.

Mastroianni turned several shades of red. Then he said, "I will do it."

Marcello Mastroianni was born in Fontana Liri in Ciociaria on September 28, 1924. He grew up in an artistic family. He had two uncles who were sculptors and another who was a painter with a studio on via Margutta. His family moved to Rome when he was a young boy and their working-class apartment was near Cinecittà. At twelve years old, he began to work as an extra, playing pirates and ragamuffins. He found it magical. At the age of eighteen he was in one of De Sica's films, *The Children Are Watching Us*. He followed the esteemed director around the set, begging him for advice. He studied to be an engineer. In 1943 he was working in Rome on the city council as a technical design assistant. When the city fell to the Germans, he was sent to a labor camp. He escaped to Venice with only a suitcase full of beans and potatoes.

Returning to Rome in 1945, he began to take acting classes at Sapienza University of Rome. One of his classmates was

Giulietta Masina. He was in a production with Giulietta in 1943, the year she married Federico. He continued to do theater, working with director Luchino Visconti, who gave him his grounding as an actor. He continued to work in theater, which he called "school time," as opposed to film, which was "vacation time," until 1956. His film work between 1949 and 1956 represented a time in Italian cinema when there was a movement from neo-realism to explorations of the bourgeoisie. When he met Federico, he was mired in a series of type-cast roles. He was yearning for a challenge.

For Federico, there was no other actress but Anita Ekberg to play the spoiled diva Sylvia. She represented one aspect of femininity and beauty writ large. He found her photo in a fashion magazine and had been aware of her for some time. He followed her antics in the press as she made her way from her native Sweden to a Hollywood career in B movies and finally to Rome. Unafraid to flaunt her Nordic beauty and sexuality and to dive into Roman nightlife, Ekberg was well known for her appearances in clubs, bars, and dance halls. She was uninhibited and supremely confident of her womanly allure. Unsure at first of the methodology of Federico Fellini, she soon grew completely enamored of the sense of fun, abandon, and artistic freedom on the set.

For his part, Mastroianni was completely unattracted to Ekberg. She reminded him of a looming Wehrmacht officer who had taken him captive during World War II.

Anouk Aimée, a French actress who played one of Mastroianni's character's lovers, was a shy, tiny woman whose face Federico found mesmerizing. In order to get her to do what he wanted, he jumped up and down behind the camera, doing dances and jigs. Her sense of bemused shock was precisely what Federico wanted. As he had since he was a child with his puppets, he found a way to get actors to do exactly what he envisioned, no matter what it took. In this case, it was a world of beauty, decadence, and a search for meaning floating above the rising phoenix of postwar Italian life—a potent combination of exuberance and spiritual vacuity.

La Dolce Vita is a series of scenes that take place in and around Rome. Marcello, the jaded journalist, moves through these scenes in a desperate journey to connect. From St. Peter's to a phony miracle to Roman nightlife to liaisons with women in his life to parties and orgies, he searches for meaning and messages, but can't seem to make sense of them.

La Dolce Vita began a relationship that was to be a lifelong one between Federico and Mastroianni. The actor didn't seem to take anything too seriously, as Giulietta had said, and he brought a natural ease and confidence to his work that delighted Federico. He seemed to understand intrinsically what Federico wanted; they had an immediate simpatico. They entertained one another between shots with stories of their amorous escapades. They shared a love of sports cars. Most of all, Mastroianni seemed to absorb whatever creative notions Federico had in his head and then execute what his director wanted with precision and grace. Mastroianni fell in love with this way of filmmaking. Federico and Piero Gherardi created the life, the look of the set and the characters, and Mastroianni was more than happy to go along for the ride. He felt both like an actor and a spectator, observing the life that swirled around him on Federico's set. They became closer as the shoot progressed, even rooming together on one location. In Mastroianni, Federico felt he had found his doppelganger. Mastroianni went to a completely new level in his work as an actor, allowing himself to confront his own deeply personal conflicts with his father and his past. Working on *La Dolce Vita* fed him as an artist and provided a whole new world of creativity. The intensity gave him a feeling of joy. Federico often told him, "This is like going off on a journey. We are castaways on a raft."

The fun Federico created on set seemed to spill onto the screen. On a typical day, groups of extras sat drinking coffee or wine, playing cards, and chatting. They knew they had been chosen from Federico's now-voluminous piles of photos. Each face was selected with meticulous care. Federico felt that faces were the essential aspect of storytelling. On other parts of the set, writers might be seen typing away on an upcoming scene, hammers pounding, constant laughter, movement, and clatter. This, for Federico, was the essence of life, the method by which he often drew out secrets and hidden truths he wished to share. More and more as he worked, the true creation happened while filming—spontaneous and fulfilling his mysterious vision.

The hallway outside his office was filled every day with visitors. They were actors, writers, lion tamers, magicians, old-time vaudevillians, hunchbacks, little people, giants, snake charmers, psychics, and some who just wanted to meet the famous director and perhaps give him a little advice. Federico said yes to all of them. He saw people without appointments. There were endless auditions, performances, and interviews, some short and some lengthy. Federico loved these people, many of whom lived on the fringes of society. He embraced them and was inspired by them.

They also all wanted something from him and he often felt inadequate to provide them with what they wanted. The constant pressures grew on him. The lack of a meaningful relationship with his recently deceased father came to him in frightening dreams; he felt himself floating, disconnected from the earth, or, worse yet, drowning just beneath the surface of the waves. At these times, Federico would lie on the sofa in his office, prostrate and full of demons, lost in his thoughts.

He was having just such a day on one blustery January evening in 1962 when there was a knock on his office door. It was the end of a long day of meetings. He had just met and heard five-year-old twin accordionists, accompanied by their stage mother.

A woman's head popped in. She resembled a friendly troll. She had a wide smile and short cropped black hair. She wore no makeup and strode into his office as though she had been there forever.

"I've arrived," she said.

Federico, who had been stretched out on his sofa, stood up. He towered over the tiny woman.

"So I see. Welcome to you. If I might ask . . . who are you?"

"Liliana. Liliana Betti. From Brescia. We've been corresponding for a year." She brought out a sheaf of letters that she had organized into a binder.

"Yes! Yes! Of course, the director," said Federico. "What took you so long?"

"No, you are the director. I just dream of being a director," she answered.

"All you need are dreams," said Federico.

"Does your office always look like this?" she asked, indicating the piles of headshots, half-read scripts that lay open, and overflowing ashtrays.

"I'm afraid so, yes," said Federico.

"And the hallway outside," she said, looking up at him. "Do you realize there is an organ grinder with a live monkey, an opera singer with her accompanist, and a man who says he is a sword swallower?"

"No, but that's typical," said Federico.

He felt immediately at ease with Betti, as though she could take care of herself. Moreover, she seemed unfazed by what many people would find bizarre; in fact, she seemed to love it. She became his personal assistant, casting assistant, and general scheduler. She ran interference with producers and the endless numbers of people who wanted to see him, ask his advice, and seek employment. She went with Federico on long rides through the streets of Rome late at night, in which the director, in constant motion, went over his ideas and plans for the next day's work.

Federico's discovery and use of the CinemaScope camera to shoot *La Dolce Vita* gave a shallow depth of field to the scenes and made it seem as though each of the characters was surrounded by, and in some cases engulfed by, the city of Rome. The characters seem to float in a nebulous world of disconnection while at the same time being in the midst of the city.

The set for *La Dolce Vita* became entertainment for Romans. Huge crowds began to gather to watch the filming. During the week of night shoots it took to film the Anita Ekberg's dip in the Trevi Fountain, thousands of spectators lined the streets; the fact that the shoot took place in the middle of the night seemed to deter no one. Onlookers surrounded the monument, catcalling, whistling, and awaiting the Nordic beauty. They were not disappointed. Ekberg, raised in Sweden and used to cold water, had no compunction about wading into the frigid March waters of the fountain dressed in a low-cut black velvet dress. Marcello Mastroianni, raised in a Mediterranean climate, needed alcoholic fortification. They couldn't have known that their fountain frolic would become one of the most iconic scenes in the history of cinema.

Federico had permission to close down via Veneto for the scenes that took place there. The crowds that gathered to watch the filming were distracting and oppressive. Federico quickly began to lose his preference for working on location, which had begun when he was a young man working with Rossellini. He insisted that via Veneto needed to be recreated at Cinecittà so that he would have control over the set. Rizzoli agreed to the cost of having Piero Gherardi do this on one condition: Federico had to relinquish his percentage of any of the film's profit and take only his director's fee, the equivalent of $50,000. In order to make the film he wanted to make, Federico agreed. The set was built.

When the shoot for *La Dolce Vita* finished in September 1959, all the actors who had worked on it felt transformed. Ekberg, who had been skeptical at first, cried when her final scene was over. She had to be gently pried away and taken to her dressing room. Mastroianni knew his inner life as an artist had been profoundly deepened and changed. He was yet to know how his entire life and career would be altered.

La Dolce Vita premiered at the Cinema Fiamma in Rome on February 3, 1960. The film had already caused a furor of controversy. The Catholic Church did not give its approval to *La Dolce Vita*. There was a parliamentary debate over the merits of the film. When it premiered in Milan on February 5 at the Cinema Capitol, some in the audience hissed and booed. As Federico was leaving the auditorium, he felt something wet at the back of his neck. Someone had spit on him. Giulietta dissolved in tears.

There was another premiere scheduled at the Cinema Capitol the following afternoon. Federico and Ennio Flaiano met for lunch at a favorite eatery just down the street from the theater. When they finished their pasta and stepped outside, they saw a massive crowd in front of the theater. They assumed that something terrible had happened. When they neared the theater, they realized it was merely the crowd massing, trying to get in. The audience was so eager, they broke a window.

Despite the controversy surrounding it, or perhaps because of the resulting publicity, *La Dolce Vita* drew crowds larger than the ones for *Ben-Hur,* the film that was the closest in box office contention. Within three months, it had grossed 15 million *lire.* In America, it took in $8 million, outgrossing any other foreign language film. The term *paparazzi* became ubiquitous. The story of the journalist in modern Rome who wandered the world but was not *of* the world, detached and increasingly aware of the difficulty of finding meaningful connection in a culture that was becoming alien, had a powerful effect on audiences. It painted a picture that was startling; a city and a culture at a crossroads. For some, it was an ugly and shocking exposé and felt like a betrayal. For others, it touched a profound note exposing the aching sense of yearning that accompanied what it felt to be alive in Rome in 1960.

The great irony was that Federico had renounced his profits from *La Dolce Vita* in order to build via Veneto at Cinecittà, so he only received $50,000 and a gold watch from his paternalistic producer, Angelo Rizzoli. The year marked Federico's fortieth birthday. At the Cannes Film Festival, presided over by writer Georges Simenon, Federico's friend and admirer, *La Dolce Vita* won the Palme d'Or by unanimous decision.

Soon, Federico would begin a new film, one that would explore the dreamlike world of an artist caught between his own inertia and the growing demands of his public. He felt compelled to explore and express the various parts of himself through his art. As Federico himself said, "I could make a film about a salmon and it would still be about me."

Chapter Eight

THE DREAM OF WOMEN

Federico dreamed he was standing at the head of a long line of impatient people waiting to board a plane. He was the head of immigration and as such had to decide who could fly and who couldn't. He couldn't make a decision about the status of an Asian man at the front of the line. The man was angry. Suddenly the dream changed and he found himself dressed in a ringmaster's hat and tails. He was standing in a room full of dirty water and snapping a whip at performing rats swimming beside him. The water was getting higher and higher. It reached his chin. He was terrified of drowning.

Federico woke with a start. He was in his own bed. Giulietta sat next to him, calmly reading. It was a book about Mother Cabrini and she hoped to convince Federico to make a film about her so that Giulietta could play the role. It would be a perfect role. She put out the cigarette she had been smoking and stretched her arms.

"You were talking in your sleep. Something about rats."

She opened the drawer in her nightstand and brought out a flat package wrapped in tissue. "I bought this for you today, Fefe."

It was a leather-bound notebook with hundreds of blank pages. The leather was exquisitely tooled. The pages were made of vellum paper.

"Dr. Bernhard told you to make drawings and sketches of your dreams. This will be your dream book. I have no doubt there will be beautiful women on each page," she said with a laugh.

Federico kissed his wife. "None as beautiful as you. I could never begin to capture your glowing essence. Besides, the first sketch will feature rats, not beautiful women. I have another problem. All this dreaming makes me hungry. I'm starving. Will you make me spaghetti?"

"But it is 1:00 a.m.!" Giulietta protested.

They both knew she would give in. No one could ever say no to Federico.

They walked into the kitchen. Giulietta lit a cigarette. It hung on her lower lip as she cut up garlic and placed the tomatoes just so in the pan. There was an American tune on the radio, a song by Frankie Avalon called "Venus." She hummed along as she cooked. Federico sat at the kitchen table totally absorbed in drawing his sketch. He was thrilled with his book of dreams. It was a rare moment of domestic bliss in a marriage between two artists who had become international icons. It had become increasingly difficult to find moments of peace.

Early in 1960 Federico had begun seeing Dr. Ernst Bernhard, a Jungian analyst. Federico had scoffed at analysis for years, but was encouraged by his friend Vittorio De Seta to try a Jungian psychologist. De Seta gave him Dr. Bernhard's phone number. Federico put it in his pocket and forgot about it. One day he mistook the number for that of an actress he wanted to call. Dr. Bernhard answered, and Federico felt it was fate pointing the way. He believed fervently in synchronicity. He began seeing Dr. Bernhard, who lived not far from the via Archimede apartment, on a regular basis. It profoundly changed the way Federico thought about his past and influenced his cinematic art for the rest of his life.

Dr. Bernhard, who had studied with Carl Jung, taught Federico about Jung's concept of individuation, the process of separating the self out of each person's conscious and subconscious. The aspects of this lifelong process—which included synchronicity, archetypal phenomena, the collective unconscious, the psychological complex, extroversion, and introversion—were all crystalized and clarified for Federico, along with Jung's emphasis on the importance of dreams.

As far back as Federico could remember, his dream life had been nearly equal in importance to his waking life. He had shame and guilt about his dreams and had repressed those feelings. Now, with Dr. Bernhard's encouragement, his dreams were seen as part of the basis for his creative life—as treasures to be cherished, nourished, and examined. His dream life, full of symbols, emotions, and archetypes, was a message from the depths of his soul that both made him who he was and connected him with the rest of humanity. Dr. Bernhard's Jungian theories, especially about the collective unconscious and its deep well of archetypal meaning, allowed Federico to examine his past life and present desires without judgment. It gave him an entirely new way of looking at the world and a whole new context for expressing it in his art. There was no need to hide or repress or ignore dreams; in fact, dream life was to be celebrated.

Federico's work with Dr. Bernhard allowed him to revel in, not cast aside, his dreams and to see them not as shameful, but as vital parts of his creativity. It encouraged him to embrace these aspects of his conscious and subconscious mind, to delve into these experiences without censure. Dr. Bernhard's grasp of both science and magic, reality and fantasy, opened a whole new world for Federico. It released him, made him more brave to not only envision, but also to communicate these parts of his life and personality.

Despite his hatred of travel, Federico made a pilgrimage to Bollingen, Switzerland, to Jung's final home on Lake Obersee. In the placid setting, Jung had built a home consisting of circular stone towers. Jung's office was in one tower and Federico was allowed to visit the inner sanctum. It was filled with ancient masks, mandalas, Tibetan symbols, paints, easels, and drawing materials—a sort of playroom for the soul. Federico began to feel that he had a great deal in common with the famous doctor: a love of magic, symbol, and ritual; a potent interest in the things that all human beings experience. In Jung's expansive view of the commonalities of humanity, Federico experienced the glory of imagination and the very real and urgent beauty of messages from the unconscious. Federico was most taken with a stone on which Jung had carved the compendium of his life philosophies in quotes. One of the inscriptions said: "Time is a child—playing like a child—playing a board game . . . He points the way to the gates of the sun and to the land of dreams." There was a saying inscribed above Jung's front door that said: "Summoned or not, God will be present." Federico was deeply moved by his visit to Bollingen.

Encouraged by Dr. Bernhard, both Federico and Giulietta began to explore paranormal life, magic, and the ancient Chinese philosophical guide *I Ching,* and to consult with famous mediums such as Gustav Rol. Astrology, alchemy, and palmistry books filled Federico's personal library at the apartment on via Archimede. They sought answers to the mysteries of life in things that were not material, but spiritual.

At the age of forty, Federico was beginning to feel his youth was behind him. In Jung, through Dr. Bernhard, he found some measure of self-acceptance. He came to understand that the only thing that exists is the true self, unencumbered by the lies, myths, and fantasies we create as subterfuge and protection. The awards and the crowds, producers, and actors all demanding, pleading, and begging for his time had become overwhelming. He had lost something that Jungian analysis seemed to replenish. The core was to be found in his own subconscious, in dream life. For the rest of his life, one of his favorite questions to friends, crew, and cast members was "How did you sleep? Did you dream?"

As the 1960s began, Angelo Rizzoli, eager to maintain an ongoing relationship with Federico, created a production company in partnership with him. It was called Federiz, a combination of their names. Their offices were decorated by

Piero Gherardi with striking green-striped curtains and ultra-modern orange sofas. An outer office featured a large table piled high with stacks of photographs of actors that Federico loved. An inner office, where Federico could hold private meetings, saw a steady stream of people who wanted to work with him. Ostensibly Federiz was created to nurture the talents and creativity of up-and-coming Italian filmmakers. Giulietta pitched her project about Mother Cabrini; his brother, Riccardo, a documentary about Sardinian fishermen; Pasolini, a screenplay and potential film produced by Federiz. Federico soon had to admit that the truth was he didn't want to work on any films but his own. The artists, including Giulietta, who had brought projects to him to be taken under his wing were summarily disappointed.

One of the people who clamored for and got Federico's attention was producer Carlo Ponti. He reminded Federico that he owed Ponti a film based on a deal they had made years before. Ponti proposed a short film to be a part of a project he was putting together that was to be a modern version of Boccaccio's *Decameron*. The other filmmakers would be De Sica, Visconti, and Morandi. Federico seized on the subject of censorship and immediately began crafting a script about a pious, unctuous doctor who prowls lover's lanes breaking up couples, snatches girlie magazines from newsstands, and demands that scantily dressed women cover themselves. He is outraged by a billboard that appears in his neighborhood, within clear view of his window. It features a recumbent woman with her breasts spilling out of her dress, admonishing people to "drink more milk." He insists that the billboard be removed and then becomes obsessed by it, dreaming of a nightmarish scenario in which the woman on the billboard comes to life and, like a giantess in a fairy tale, chases him. He ends up ignominiously prostrate, half naked atop the billboard, and is ultimately hauled away, presumably to an asylum.

Federico hired the comedic actor Peppino De Filippo as the lead. He enticed Anita Ekberg to come back to Rome to play the woman from the billboard who comes to life. Now an international star, Ekberg was no longer so easygoing and pliable. Nonetheless, the shoot was a sort of holiday for Federico and it marked two important new aspects of his filmmaking: the use of color and the use of dream sequences. Although used mainly to comedic effect in *The Temptation of Dr. Antonio,* the dream sequences heralded the beginning of a whole new way of thinking about storytelling and character.

Night drives before and during *The Temptation of Dr. Antonio* became an ever more essential part of Federico's work life. He had a notion for his next film and used the nocturnal excursions to flesh out his ideas. Sometimes he took others with him on his nighttime drives, including Lina Wertmüller, who had been introduced to Federico by Marcello Mastroianni and became a close colleague. She was a native-born Roman and had come from the world of theater and puppetry. Her desire was to become a filmmaker. She and Federico were immediately simpatico and he took her on as an assistant director.

Liliana Betti had become Federico's right-hand assistant, working with him on casting, script supervision, and all parts of film production. Federico began calling her "the boss" and "the little goddess of ideas." Betti also accompanied Federico on his evening crawls, as did Piero Gherardi, Tullio Pinelli, and Ennio Flaiano, depending on what aspect of the project Federico wanted to discuss that night.

Angelo Rizzoli began to ready the production at his Scalera Studios, although there was still no finished script. Federico knew that he needed a spaceship, yet he couldn't explain why. He asked for one to be constructed.

Federico began to detail his ideas for the film to Pinelli, Flaiano, and Brunello Rondi. It would be the story of a man in midlife crisis, not sure of himself. He would be a character plagued with demons, full of memories of the past and current pressures from which he wants to escape. He is surrounded by women: his wife, his mistress, his mother, a young woman who represents purity and sweetness. He is at times responsive and at times just wants to escape them all.

Pinelli was doubtful it was a story. Rondi, as usual, was more supportive. The always skeptical Flaiano vetoed it outright. The script nonetheless began to take shape, fleshed out during nightly drives around Rome. Gossip columnists and journalists begged for tidbits about the new Fellini film, but the developing script was kept under lock and key.

As characters began to emerge and the casting process began, Federico was besieged with calls from all over Europe and America. Producers, managers, and agents around the world called to propose their clients for the film. Never satisfied with only casting well-known stars, Federico sought out fascinating faces from his past as well as new and unusual actors, some of whom had never been in a film before and some who were cast just because of their appearance. Federico put an advertisement in papers in Rome, Milan, and Turin that said: "Do you have a Rubenesque body? Do you look like you could have been painted by Titian? Do you have a shape like a cello? Then Fellini might want you!" It gave an address, usually a large piazza, and a date and time. Lina Wertmüller and Liliana Betti were sent to sort through the thousands of women who showed up for the casting calls. All the photos of persons of interest were saved and added to the stacks in Federico's office. If they weren't used in this film, they were sure to be considered for a future project.

Federico's unusual casting methods were on display when he burst into Sandra Milo's apartment early one morning with Piero Gherardi and Gianni Di Venanzo to do makeup and lighting for an impromptu screen test. Milo, who had been hesitating about playing the scatterbrained mistress, gave in. As he was leaving the apartment, Federico insisted that she gain at least ten pounds in order to have the zaftig appearance he conceived for her character. She had just struggled to lose weight. But she agreed to everything. No one, it seemed, could refuse Federico Fellini.

At one point in January 1963, Federico flew to New York City to speak to Laurence Olivier about the possibility of playing the lead. Marcello Mastroianni also happened to be in New York City, as he was being courted by Arthur Miller to be the lead in his play *After the Fall*. Federico finally made his decision. The lead would be played by Marcello. None of his collaborators were the least bit surprised. They had known from the beginning that it would be Mastroianni. The opera singer Eddra Gale, whom Federico had seen on the street in Rome, would play the seductress Saranghina; the beautiful up-and-coming starlet Claudia Cardinale would play the symbol of womanly purity; Anouk Aimée was cast as the long-suffering wife.

As a part of research for the screenplay, the first scene of which was set in a spa, Federico and Tullio Pinelli spent ten days at the Chianciano Terme spa. Set against the backdrop of the Val di Chiana mountains, the spa had been in use for millennia. The Etruscans had built a temple at the source, and since ancient times, people of all ages and states had come to take dips in the healing pools, drink cups of water from the mineral springs that were thought to heal all manner of ills, and to take treatments. Doctors, nurses, and healers of all kinds buzzed around the clientele, who varied from the wealthiest industrialists to bishops and priests from the local church.

The production plans hummed along, the cast was close to being finalized, and sets were being built at Scalera Studios in Rome. The script was being revised daily. But still Federico could not think of an occupation for the lead character. A sense of malaise took over his soul. He felt blocked, unable to complete the script and incapable of meeting the demands placed on him.

Meanwhile, Giulietta was in France making a film with Jacques Duvivier. She had told Federico that she was being asked to do a nude scene in a bathtub. Federico was furious and jealous. He felt alone and miserable, although he hid his feelings from the staff in the production offices. In mid-April 1963, he decided he couldn't go on. He wrote a letter to Rizzoli letting him know he was quitting the production and apologizing for his ineptitude. He walked out of his office and saw Wertmüller and Betti poring over photographs, considering actors for the smaller roles.

It was lunchtime and Federico was summoned to the stage where the set was being built. One of the electricians, Gasparino, was celebrating a birthday. The crew raised glasses of Spumante. One was thrust into Federico's hand. They toasted the birthday boy, who had been working all morning rigging lights under the exacting direction of Gianni Di Venanzo. Then the entire crew turned toward Federico and raised their glasses to him. "To the Maestro!" they all said in unison.

Federico looked into their expectant faces, so many of them familiar from other shoots. Some were very young and had spoken to him about making their own films. The seamstresses stood in their cloth slippers, happy to take a break from their sewing machines and sip bubbly. Giuseppe, the crew caterer, had a war injury and limped from one crewmember to another, refilling glasses. Rizzoli stood in the doorway to the soundstage, counting the bottles of Spumante.

Federico plastered on a smile and bowed to all of them. He understood that these cinema gypsies were his family. They were his responsibility, whether he wanted it or not. And he knew at that moment that the occupation of the leading character would be that of a director, a film director at a moment of life crisis.

He looked at the lineup of faces as they stood against the partially constructed set—a spaceship to nowhere. There were young people barely out of their teens, reminiscent of the young man he had been, stepping onto the train in Rimini over twenty years ago. There were people whose wizened faces had seen two World Wars and begun their lives when horses were still the main mode of transportation. They were his adopted family. They all needed something from him. He would try to be a hero. He would try to accommodate them all. And from them, he in turn would demand the best they had to give. He would not abandon the ship.

Despite misgivings on the part of his co-writers, complaints about production cost overruns, and the usual back-and-forth with final casting, the film began shooting on May 16, 1963. It was now called *8½* to represent the eight films Federico had directed, plus the film he co-directed with Lattuada, *Variety Lights.*

The film opens in the midst of a nightmare. It is soundless. Guido, the leading character, is caught in a traffic jam. He sees people from his life in adjoining cars. The car begins to fill with noxious gas. Then, suddenly, he is on the edge of a cliff, only saved from plunging into the sea by a thin cord wrapped around his ankle, which is anchored by a grip from the film set that surrounds him. He is rescued only by awakening, where he is being examined by doctors at the spa to which he retreated to hopefully heal and remove his creative block.

The rest of the story details the relationships in his life: the scatterbrained mistress, his increasingly estranged wife, his mother, the young woman who represents innocence, the prostitute Saranghina, hordes of would-be actresses and actors, and, of course, anxious producers and writers. As Guido attempts to come to terms with his inability to move forward creatively, he is besieged by past memories and present needs.

With *8½*, Federico had full confidence that the journey between dream and reality could be utterly fluid. There was no longer a need for a line of demarcation. There was one complete script on the set, usually held by Liliana Betti. None of the actors ever saw it. Instead, they were given their lines on set. With Sandra Milo, Marcello Mastroianni, Anouk Aimée, and the entire cast, Federico had assembled actors who were willing to give themselves over to the moment and to put their work completely into his hands. They loved and respected him and found in this way of working a sense of complete freedom. Scenes shifted and changed, but always with the give-and-take between the director and his actors.

Betti, Federico's right-hand assistant, and Lina Wertmüller, the neophyte filmmaker, continued to intuit Federico's needs. During their night crawls to clear his head after the long days of shooting, they would often stop in front of St. Peter's Square and look up at the window that he imagined was the residence of Pope John XXIII. Although Federico had endless censorship battles, he also counted many friends among the Church, including Angelo Arpa. When he saw a light in the window, he said it gave him reassurance to know the pope was there.

Federico was totally absorbed in the making of *8½*, as with every film he made, and was most alive when in the process of shooting. The film brought together his relationships with women, the conflicts over duty to oneself versus others, and the responsibility of the artist in society.

While shooting a trailer to advertise the film, Federico decided to bring together the whole cast—everyone who had appeared in the film. They walked down a huge stairway with a circus parade and the haunting melody of a tune composed by Nino Rota. The ringmaster's final words are "Life is a holiday; let us live it together." A small boy who leads the parade is the final image of the film. It seemed to sum up Federico's wish for those viewing the film and for his own life—the joy he found in working, in creating, in living.

Critics, as usual, were divided in their response to Fellini's film. Audiences were not. They packed the cinemas throughout Italy to see *8½,* and many saw it multiple times.

Federico went to work almost immediately on a film expressly created for Giulietta. The film was titled *Juliet of the Spirits* and was ostensibly about a middle-aged woman with a philandering husband who yearns for a surcease to her loneliness and feelings of abandonment. Many who worked on the film, including the writers, felt it was uncomfortably close to the realities that existed in the marriage between Federico and Giulietta. It was the first feature film that Federico had directed in color. Piero Gherardi was given free rein to create costumes and set designs whose geometric shapes and sheer size seemed to dwarf the actors. The set of *Juliet of the Spirits,* like many films before it, became a sort of tourist destination for visiting celebrities, royalty, and fellow artists who wanted to see the "maestro" at work. Lunches and elaborate dining rooms were often built next to the sets to accommodate these visitors.

For her part, Giulietta, the star of the film, had now experienced a series of films with other directors that had not been successful. She had also given up a significant amount of time and energy to help her husband with his career. *Juliet of the Spirits* was to be a gift from Federico to his wife—a chance for them to work together again.

The difficulties began almost immediately with the shift from black and white to color film. Fellini's cinematographer and friend Gianni Di Venanzo, the undisputed genius of black and white, was at odds and out of his element working with color. Most disturbing, Giulietta and Federico had major disagreements about the themes of the film. Their arguments reflected their differing personalities and ways of looking at life. Federico was interested in exploring the mystical side of the life of the leading character, an aging woman with an unfaithful husband. Giulietta wanted to explore the reality. Federico's co-writers, Pinelli and Flaiano, began to feel increasingly alienated.

During the shoot, Federico and Giulietta built a summer house based on a design from *Juliet of the Spirits* in the beach town of Fregene, outside of Rome. They had dinner parties at their white stucco villa. Invitations to these soirées were highly sought after. American and Italian celebrities feasted on pasta dishes Giulietta cooked; after dinner, charades were played. Close observers felt some of the gaiety was forced. Federico rarely participated.

The critical response to *Juliet of the Spirits* was not positive.

The experience of making the film, which was particularly arduous, was made all the more torturous by the sudden death of Di Venanzo, who died of hepatitis not long after the film was finished. Federico's relationship with Pinelli and Flaiano was strained. He felt exhausted by the tepid response to *Juliet of the Spirits,* betrayed by friends, and deeply saddened by the death of Di Venanzo.

The mood was mitigated somewhat by the Academy Award nomination for Best Foreign Language Film for *8½.* Angelo Rizzoli planned a trip to Los Angeles that would include Federico, Giulietta, Mastroianni, Gherardi, and Flaiano. When they began to board the plane and Flaiano realized that he was the only member of the party who had not been placed in first class, the frustrations, irritations, and professional slights he believed he had endured all came to the surface. He completely broke down, but was finally calm enough to board the plane. Federico explained that he had nothing to do with the seating and attempted to smooth things over by sitting with his longtime friend and collaborator. But the damage was done. The friendship had been undermined and the compatibility shattered.

On the night of April 13, 1964, Federico accepted the Academy Award for Best Foreign Language Film for *8½.* He gave a short speech. He was focused on the thought that perhaps this award would allow him to make more films.

Federico realized, more than ever, that his films were his children, his life. The trip to Hollywood, with the glitz and the ludicrous nature of its hype, mystified him. He despised travel and anything that took him away from his beloved city of Rome.

"Making a movie is a vacation," he said to Giulietta as they returned from Los Angeles to Rome. "All the rest—publicity, premieres—is the work. I am going to go to sleep now. And when I sleep, I will dream of my films."

Federico and Giulietta were devastated when, on their return to Rome, they found out that the young actor who had played Guido as a little boy in *8½* had died suddenly.

Giulietta and Federico were now middle-age artists, internationally famous, arguably one of the most successful couples in cinematic history. They had a beautiful apartment in Rome and a summer house in Fregene. The Oscar statuette went into the room where they kept their awards. It represented work in the past. There was no way to escape aging; everyone alive would eventually die. The only thing to renew the life force was a creative future. Federico plunged ahead.

Chapter Nine

THE DREAM OF DEATH

Federico could not stop thinking about death. The words of the producer at the end of *8½* kept ringing through his head: "If you don't finish this film, I'll ruin you." Who had thought of that dialogue? Flaiano, probably. The film ended on a high note, with an expression of joy and life-affirming unity: the entire cast dancing together in a celebration of life and love. Federico was no longer so certain of the joy in life. Despite the awards and the recognition of *8½*, a fair amount of critics had savaged *Juliet of the Spirits*. Federico had meant it to be a tribute to his wife. But things had not turned out well. The team of writers with whom he had created for over a decade were now barely speaking to him. Piero Gherardi, stung by the criticism of his overbearing costume design in *Juliet of the Spirits* and exhausted by the frantic pace of working with Federico, had decided he had done his final film for the maestro. Gianni Di Venanzo, the brilliant cinematographer with whom Federico had worked for nearly a decade, was dead. Giulietta, disappointed and confused by the mixed response to the film, felt both angered and humiliated.

She retreated to the house in Fregene as a respite from the constant media spotlight in Rome.

Among the producers who continued to pursue Federico, Dino De Laurentiis was chief among them. De Laurentiis had given up Federico to producer Angelo Rizzoli for long enough. He was not about to lose out again. He was eager to hear Federico's idea for his next film.

In a meeting at De Laurentiis's office in his Dinocittà studios, Federico expounded on an idea that had been in his dreams for years. He looked around the room, ruefully taking in the satin-covered sofas and gigantic bouquets of flowers—the opulence of a successful producer. He decided to proceed with his pitch knowing that De Laurentiis would probably be skeptical.

"A man is nearing the end of a long plane flight," Federico began. "The plane has trouble landing but finally succeeds. When he exits, it is into a surreal world of fog, grayness, and ashes. He finds himself in a huge square near a cathedral and sees strange figures and sights. It begins to dawn on him that perhaps the plane didn't actually land safely and that he has in fact died. He begins to meet people from throughout his life, parents and grandparents, all kinds of ancestors who greet him warmly. He journeys through various worlds that touch on different aspects of his life. Finally he sees his wife, happily remarried."

Federico went on to describe the sets that would have to be built, among them a huge plaza; a cathedral resembling one he had seen in Cologne, Germany; a life-size jet plane; and locations that would vary from London to Paris to New York City.

The budget would be the equivalent of over $1 million, and a quarter of that would be his salary.

Although De Laurentiis found the outline meandering, he agreed to the project and put his brother, Luigi, in charge. De Laurentiis was willing to take the gamble on the internationally famous director, providing the right star could be found to play the lead. On this point, he would not budge.

Federico, along with his assistant Liliane Betti and members of his team, was installed at Dinocittà studios. From the moment he entered the lot, Federico began to have second thoughts about the project. In the world of De Laurentiis, who was just completing the premiere of the behemoth film *The Bible,* Federico felt like just another worker. He felt displaced and disoriented. One day, while resting on the sofa in his office, Federico experienced a horrifying hallucination. Bricks from a building crashed down on him, suffocating him. He was unable to escape. He awoke, frantically thrashing, and found himself on the floor six feet away from the sofa. He had no idea how he had gotten there. These and other omens began to cripple him creatively.

On June 29, 1965, as Federico began to struggle to put together a team for what he now was calling *The Voyage of G. Mastorna,* he received word that his beloved Dr. Ernst Bernhard had died suddenly. It was a devastating blow. In the nearly five years Federico had spent with Dr. Bernhard, he had found a father figure, someone whose belief in the potent combination of science and mysticism had opened Federico to a renewed sense of himself. With this loss, Federico felt alone and bereft.

Meanwhile, Giulietta began a radio advice show that became wildly popular. It kept her in the public eye in a new and vital way. The notion that the public at large could get advice from the actress who had played Gelsomina and Cabiria was appealing. The idea that they could share their sorrows and joys with the actress who had just played Juliet, a middle-aged woman dealing with a straying husband, proved irresistible; thousands of listeners poured their hearts out to her, wrote letters, and sought her help. Giulietta didn't have all the answers, but she felt for each of them.

Federico continued to struggle with *The Voyage of G. Mastorna.* He found a writer, the eminent novelist and journalist Dino Buzzati. Federico's long preferred way of working through story ideas—driving in his sports car around Rome and environs at all hours, usually in the middle of the night—would not work for Buzzati, who lived in Milan, had a family, and was not amenable to late-night jaunts. He had never written a screenplay before. He and Federico struggled to work together and finally gave up.

On September 14, 1966, Federico decided he could go no further. That day, he had visited the set on which an enormous Gothic cathedral had been built. He saw the shell of a huge jumbo jet, still under construction. It sat, awaiting completion and a cast and crew to fill it. Gustavo Rol, Federico's personal psychic, had warned him not to continue with the project. Federico sat down to write a letter of resignation to Dino De Laurentiis. In it, he outlined his inability to go on with the project. He apologized profusely.

Federico and Giulietta left for their summer home in Fregene to sequester themselves from the media storm they knew would follow. They didn't predict, however, that De Laurentiis would take swift legal action. Within two weeks, De Laurentiis and his team of lawyers filed a lawsuit for damages. They demanded repayment of Federico's salary plus all expenses for set construction and pre-production. Officers arrived at their Fregene home and began confiscating valuable paintings, including a Renoir, in order to punish Federico. To make matters worse, the right-wing government began cracking down on tax evaders. They began to focus on high-profile celebrities, and Marcello Mastroianni, Sophia Loren, and Federico were all faced with huge tax bills. Fortunately, the ever-practical Giulietta had put many of their assets in her name. Because of this, their home in Fregene was spared.

At the beginning of January 1967, Federico and De Laurentiis met on a foggy day in the Borghese Gardens to try a reconciliation. They arrived in separate black town cars surrounded by phalanxes of lawyers, awaiting a hopeful outcome. The two men were equally skilled at bluster and mental marksmanship. They walked along the manicured pathways. The garden was deserted on the early winter morning. Federico, tall and now heavy, towered over the diminutive De Laurentiis. The two men, the artist and the producer, had been locked in a battle of wits for over a decade. After almost an hour, the meeting was concluded with a hug. The lawyers took this as a good sign and went to work on renewed contracts and agreements.

Within weeks, Federico was once again ensconced in an

office paid for by De Laurentiis, fielding offers from agents and managers all over the world for the lead in his new film. Once again, he had a sinking feeling. De Laurentiis pushed popular Italian actor Ugo Tognazzi because he had box office appeal. Beaten down, Federico reluctantly agreed. The nightmares returned, many of them involving planes that crashed and signs saying "halt." Federico dutifully sketched them in his dream book.

Federico and Giulietta moved closer to Dinocittà, into the Grand Hotel in Rome's EUR, a neighborhood that was an ugly reminder of the Mussolini era. On the evening of April 10, 1967, Giulietta went out to see a film. Federico was not feeling well. His mental state deteriorated when he happened to see *La Strada* on television, followed by a negative critique. He despised the idea of films being shown on television, a medium for which they were not made. Federico began to feel shortness of breath and heart palpitations. He called for the hotel doctor, who happened to be attending an elegant soirée in the lobby. The doctor came to Federico dressed in a top hat and tails, gave him a shot of antibiotics, and returned to the party. Federico attempted to get up a few minutes later and collapsed on the floor.

Hotel employees found him, called the doctor, and within minutes Federico was being hauled down the stairs and through the middle of the party on the shoulders of hotel employees. The doctor himself drove Federico to the hospital. Federico was half awake, lying on the back seat, when he heard a crash. They had gotten into an accident. He heard the doctor say, "You have to let me go. I have a dying man in the back." The car sped to the hospital with Federico prone on the cold leather seat, looking up at the surreal night of Rome: neon signs, flashing traffic lights, glimpses of billboards, the tops of buildings both ancient and modern.

News of his illness made international headlines. Dino De Laurentiis, suspicious that Federico was somehow faking to get out of directing *The Voyage of G. Mastorna,* sent his own team of doctors. They concurred that the illness was real and said they suspected cancer. The doctors at the Salvator Mundi clinic thought it was a severe case of pleurisy and continued to give him antibiotics.

The nurses at Salvator Mundi were also nuns. Their presence both frightened and comforted Federico. The room filled with flowers, the most beautiful of which were from Angelo Rizzoli, who claimed he was in a constant state of tears. Even Ennio Flaiano visited. When he departed, Federico said to the ever-vigilant Giulietta, who never left his side at the hospital, "If Flaiano came, now I know I must be dying." The pope himself sent a greeting and a wish for his recovery. Federico marveled at this, given the checkered history of his censorship battles with the Catholic Church.

The most vocal and insistent visitors were his friends from Rimini. They refused to be turned away. Titta Benzi and Ettore Scola, an old friend who had become a doctor, indignantly pushed their way inside on the third day of Federico's stay. Scola took one look at Federico's chart and pronounced his definitive diagnosis: a rare disease called Sanarelli-Schwartzmann. Because he worked in a laboratory, he recognized the symptoms of a rare immune reaction. Although it took much convincing, Scola finally got the doctors to administer cortisone. Federico began to breathe more easily immediately. Within twenty-four hours he began to feel like himself again. Because of his dislike of the choice De Laurentiis had forced on him as the lead in *The Voyage of G. Mastorna,* Federico took to calling his illness "Tognazzitis."

As part of his recovery and because seeing his friends reminded him of his hometown, Federico decided to go there for a prolonged visit. In the hospital, he had many dreams about Rimini—the gray marbled sea, the port around which hotels and caffès were set. He wanted to see Ida and Maddalena, who now had a family of her own. The visit and the suggestion by a friend that Federico write down his memories of Rimini prompted the publication of the memoir with photographs. It was called *La Mia Rimini.* Dredging up memories of his youth in Rimini planted the seeds for a future film.

Rimini had changed and grown from the near total rubble after the incessant bombing during World War II. It was now populated with fifteen hundred hotels and boarding houses, dance halls, and bars that catered to the ever-increasing hordes of tourists. On the outskirts of town, where peasants once lived and farms once existed, there was development as far as the eye could see. It was good to be in the company of old friends like Titta, who treated him like Fefe, not an international star.

In late May of 1967, Federico was nearing the end of his sojourn in Rimini. He felt renewed by his visit, although mystified at times by the changes wrought in twenty years. On his final evening in Rimini, he took a drive to clear his head. He tried to prepare himself for what lay ahead in Rome. *The Voyage of G. Mastorna* still loomed.

Two young hitchhikers stood at the edge of the road leading out of Rimini. They were dressed in youthful counterculture costumes of the day: long hair, beads, feathers, and fringed vests. They were headed for a dance club at the edge of town. Federico picked them up. They were polite and grateful. They stepped from the car and into a club that seemed to have been built in a tent in a field at the edge of town. There was a sign above the entrance that said "The Other World." It seemed to Federico an appropriate name. His curiosity got the best of him.

He got out of his car, followed the thumping music, and peered inside. It was a huge tent with a dirt floor. He thought momentarily of the circuses of his childhood. Perhaps one of them had been right here. There were hundreds of young people dancing. Others sat cross-legged at the sides of the dance floor. Some held their partners in romantic embraces. They wore velveteen pants and miniskirts. Many wore leather sandals. Others were barefoot. This, then, was current Riminese youth. They both were and were not like the *vitellone* of Federico's youth. Like Federico, they had grown up in Rimini. They had never known the constriction of Fascism or the terror of Nazi tyranny. What gave them their sense of freedom and life? Federico was fascinated to know.

He returned to Rome and languished in his office during the summer of 1967. He continued to contemplate how to rid himself of *The Voyage of G. Mastorna*. It hung over him like a shroud. One day a man appeared in Federico's office and introduced himself as Alberto Grimaldi. Federico knew of him as he had just successfully produced one of the most popular films of the year, *The Good, the Bad, and the Ugly*. Grimaldi wanted to expand his producing repertoire and was willing to do almost anything to work with someone who had a reputation like Federico Fellini. Trained as a lawyer, Grimaldi had immediately seen the potential for making money in the film business, provided one made the right choices. His work with the director Sergio Leone on what came to be known as "spaghetti westerns" had paid off handsomely. The profits from those films put Grimaldi in a position to buy out the *Mastorna* contract by paying off De Laurentiis. De Laurentiis was so grateful he fell to his knees praising the saints for saving him, finally, from *The Voyage of G. Mastorna*.

The partnership with Alberto Grimaldi allowed Federico freedom. He was offered the chance to make a short film based on the Edgar Allan Poe story "Never Bet the Devil Your Head." It would be a part of a series of short films, all based on Poe stories. It was the first time Federico had made a film based on a work of literature. He worked with screenwriter Bernardo Zapponi. The film bore little resemblance to the Poe story with the exception of the severed head at the conclusion, and the devil, in the guise of a smirking little girl, who lures a man to his death. In Federico's hands, the film became a travelogue through the drugged-out mind of the leading character, Toby Dammit, a dissolute actor who is being brought to Rome to star in a film. Through his jaded eyes, the actor deals with menacing paparazzi, whom he physically attacks, and a nightmarish ride through Rome exhibiting the grandeur of the Coliseum juxtaposed with the garish traffic jams of modern Roman life. He endures a bizarre awards ceremony and is goaded into coming onstage to perform the "Out, out, brief candle" speech of Macbeth. He collapses and escapes to a waiting Ferrari, promised to him by his producer.

The final ten minutes of the film are Toby Dammit's hair-raising drive through the streets of nighttime Rome. He races around curves, crashing into ghostly mannequins and coming upon endless dead ends. He reaches a bridge that is out, but decides to speed recklessly forward. A wire stretched across the bridge severs his head. The devil, dressed as a blond girl in a pristine pinafore, smiles while blithely picking up his head as if it were a bouncing ball.

Federico cast Terrence Stamp, a young English actor whose reputation for dissolute behavior came close to that of the character he was to play. He arrived in Rome with little knowledge of the script, no real sense of what he was about to do, and without a word of Italian. He was plunged immediately into the first scene to be shot: the foggy, moody, final middle-of-the-night scene in which Toby Dammit dies in his Ferrari. Federico shook his hands, hugged him, and said, through an interpreter, "You've just spent all night at a party, making love to women, men, everyone; you've taken every drug known to mankind . . . now . . . action!"

To his credit, Stamp dove into the surreal experience and put himself completely in the maestro's hands. For him, as for many actors, it was a life-changing experience. Federico was completely on the actor's side—encouraging, suggesting, creating as they went along, enjoying each take, each moment. In the evenings, after the day's work was done, they had long dinners filled with laughter. Stamp had also worked with the Italian director Antonioni, an entirely different personality. Whereas Antonioni was cool, removed, and intellectual, Federico was warm, witty, full of charm and humor, accessible.

At the turn of the new year, in 1968, Federico was approached by an American documentary filmmaker who wanted to create a film about Federico's working methods, his art, the poeticism of his films. Peter Goldfarb, the director, envisioned it as a straight-ahead interview film, but the American producers had not counted on the vision and personality of their subject. Federico himself took over the film. He created a personal and stunningly rendered portrait, that of an artist taking a bird's-eye view of his past and his present, all within the context of his beloved city of Rome. Federico appeared in the film, asking questions and exploring. The finished film weaves together the present with counterculture flower children discovered on the decaying set of the unrealized *The Voyage of G. Mastorna*. It veers into the subterranean underground of the Appia Antica, and takes a visit to Marcello Mastroianni's actual home. Marcello auditions for the role of Mastorna and ultimately states, "If you had faith in this film, you would see me as the character. But you have no faith. You are scared."

The final sequence of the film is one that displays accurately the stream of visitors who frequently visit Federico, asking him to hire them to be in his films. One woman plays the accordion and sings an ancient Roma melody. Another touts her son, who can squeak like a squirrel. A third is an older actress who scolds Federico for "casting the same tired old faces." Federico patiently sees them all, lets them perform, and then says, "I am so fond of these characters who are always chasing me. They need me, but I need them more. They have such rich human qualities."

Toby Dammit and this film, called *A Director's Notebook,* allowed Federico to express the state in which he found himself when he was nearly fifty: an internationally known artist to whom freedom, in all its forms, could best be explored and understood through his deeply personal cinematic world. As his personal history unfurled, he became more and more interested in Roman history. He wanted to explore cinematically the comparisons between ancient and modern Romans. He chose *The Satyricon,* written by Petronius, one of the first Roman novelists, as the basis for his new work.

As the decade was nearing an end, Federico and Giulietta sold their elegant apartment in the Parioli neighborhood and moved to a more modest apartment in via Margutta. A charming, winding street in the center of Rome, just off the Piazza del Popolo in the Campo Marzio district, the street had long been home to artists and craftspeople. Via Margutta was simple and inviting, redolent of the artists who lived and worked there.

On their first morning in via Margutta, they walked together to buy coffee and newspapers. They discovered a fountain at the end of the street that had the masks of tragedy and comedy carved into the base. Giulietta touched the faces.

"For good luck, Fefe," she said. "I could swear they are winking at me."

"I hope it's the mask of comedy," said Federico. "Give him an extra rub. We could use some luck."

They walked slowly down via Margutta, savoring the smells of coffee roasting and tomato sauces being simmered for lunches. Federico realized, with a start, that they were walking by the pharmacy in which he had hidden nearly twenty-five years before. It had been redesigned. A young man stood outside, smoking. He had long hair and wore a beaded headband. The shop was open and the radio inside was playing "Azzurra," a popular song.

The young man waved to them and began singing along to the song. "I'm looking for a summer all year-round, and suddenly, here it is . . . ."

Federico tightened his hold on his wife's hand. They got their coffee and three newspapers. They headed back to their apartment on Via Margutta and made their way up the stairs to the second floor. They walked past the room they had already designated as the trophy corner. Statues, statuettes, plaques, and letters of citation filled the room. Federico shut the door. The apartment was not as elegant or expansive as the one in Parioli, but it embraced them. For the moment they were not internationally known celebrities. They were young lovers retreating to their Roman pied-à-terre.

Chapter Ten

THE DREAM OF HISTORY

Giulietta and Federico sat on two beach chairs. They faced toward the setting sun, letting the waves of the sea wash against their toes. It was the end of May, 1969. The crew was setting up the final shot of the day on the set of Federico's film *Satyricon.* The cast and crew were on location on the island of Ponza. The sun was beginning to set. A cold breeze had come up. Giulietta clutched a blanket around her shoulders. The sun was like an egg yolk perched on the edge of the horizon, ready to sink behind the gray clouds that arose at the day's end. Federico tapped his foot and pulled his hat down over his eyes. He knew that the producer, Alberto Grimaldi, and his team of assistants would be at their table totaling up the day's receipts. They were behind schedule and just about to lose the light. Giulietta tried to be calm, but as always, she picked up on her husband's frustration.

Federico looked behind him. The sight gave him great pleasure despite the tension. Scattered about on the beach were over two hundred people. The grips and camera operators and makeup assistants were wearing pants and jackets. The cast wore togas, string leather thongs held together by rope, and diaphanous tunics that revealed naked bodies underneath. They played cards and lay on their backs to catch the sun's last rays. Many ate from parts of box lunches they had saved, knowing the shoot would go late. They were relaxed and casual with one another as only a film company in their fifth month of work together can be. Max Born, the angelic-looking actor playing the role of Gitone, was strumming his guitar and singing a Bob Dylan song. The words floated out over the beach: "I'm a thinkin' and a wonderin' walking down the road. I once loved a woman—a child, I'm told. I gave her my heart but she wanted my soul. Don't think twice, it's all right."

Federico hummed along as he walked up the beach, teasing the actors. He placated the actress Capucine, who was worried about her makeup, and reassured another actor that he looked fine with the glass eye that Piero Tosi, the designer, had given him. Another actor, an extra, asked whether she could do a little dance during the next shot.

"Yes, my dear, but keep it simple," Federico replied.

They were like his children. They had been gathered after months and months of casting calls beginning in September of 1968. Federico had made the usual entreaties to American stars like Mae West and Charlie Chaplin, but in the end had put together a cast yielded from the streets of London, the cast of the musical *Hair,* and friends and colleagues, including the owner of one of his favorite restaurants, Mario Romagnoli, who played Trimalcione, the wealthy man who puts on a bacchanal. All of the faces in the film were striking. Many were grotesque and made more so by the elaborate hair and makeup designs.

Petronius's novel *The Satyricon* had been in Federico's consciousness since he was a teenager studying Latin. Written by one of Nero's courtiers in the first century, only a fourth of the episodic tale was extant. In Fellini's version, the story's narrator, Encolpio, who sometimes participates and sometimes stands outside the story, is in love with the young slave boy Gitone. Encolpius has a friend, Ascilto, who steals Gitone. The three attend a Roman bacchanalian feast given by Trimalcione, are captured as slaves, find a suicide, battle a Minotaur, and discover a fertility goddess. Along the way they encounter ancient Rome in all its excess as filtered through the lens of Federico Fellini. Many years ago, when Federico was the owner of the Funny Face Shop, he was asked to make drawings for a published version of the story; a rival illustrator eventually won the job. But he had never forgotten it.

Alberto Grimaldi was sold on producing the film. Federico and his co-writer, Bernardino Zapponi, spent seven months researching, speaking with historians, and hearing from weighty academicians. Liliane Betti compiled notebooks filled with sketches, photos, articles, and interviews. But in truth, Federico was writing a film with Zapponi and designing it with Danilo Donati. In the end, it bore no resemblance to historical fact or research. It was, as Federico explained, a science fiction based on frescoes and dredged up from the deep subconscious of his own mind.

He had found and was inspired by Donati, a designer who,

like Nino Rota, seemed to be able to intuit and manifest on a physical realm Federico's dreams and visions. A veteran designer from theater and opera, Donati created sets that were distinctive in their gray, ochre, and orange palette. Piero Tosi designed makeup with pastels, gold, and pale green accents that complemented the phantasmagorical look of the film. When all the elements were combined, the world that was presented was not like any other ever seen onscreen. Props used in the feast were both fantastic and practical. A large pig brought in on a huge tray had a head that hinged open, spilling out offal, links of sausage, and sweetmeats that are gobbled up by greedy guests.

Pippo Spoletini, a casting director hired solely to find and cast "special people," scoured factories, brothels, theaters, churches, and nearly every street in Rome to find the collection of striking faces and bodies that populated the film. The music was put together from African and Middle Eastern atonal compositions. The main characters were homosexual, but they were not judged or castigated. They were presented without comment. The whole effect was to create not a world of ancient Rome as formerly imagined by academics, but a living, breathing otherworld replete with desire, excess, hunger that cannot be satiated. Nearly every corner of every frame of the film was packed with something unusual, often grotesque, but always arresting visually.

Federico committed to the film with all of his being. He felt a renewed energy. He had an apartment on the lot at Cinecittà and often stayed there overnight. He rarely slept more than four hours at a time. He preferred shooting at Cinecittà as he had more control over the environment. The only time they left the studio was to shoot at Ponza Island. Federico said he had asked the producers to bring the ocean to Cinecittà, but they refused.

Federico included Ettore Bevilacqua, a personal trainer, in his entourage. He insisted Federico eat only lean meats, fruits, and vegetables. He worked out with Federico each morning. Or at least, Bevilacqua worked out while Federico often watched. Nevertheless, the diet plan paid off and Federico lost weight. He stopped smoking—a habit he and Giulietta had shared for nearly thirty years. He became zealous about it and insisted Giulietta stop as well. When she refused, they had to designate one room of their apartment as the smoking room. Federico also added a press secretary, Mario Longardi, to handle the never-ending array of invitations, requests, interviews, and pleas for his attendance at ceremonies and engagements.

Satyricon premiered at the Venice Film Festival on September 4, 1969. Tickets to the event were scalped for the equivalent of over one hundred dollars. The demand was so high they had to add another screening. Federico and Giulietta attended together and were in fine form. They held press conferences, greeted well-wishers, and answered the usual questions. At the conclusion of the nearly three-hour premiere, the audience seemed stunned. They had never seen anything like *Satyricon.* Unlike all previous premieres, when responses from critics came quickly, the response to *Satyricon* was more measured. No one could deny that with *Satyricon,* Federico Fellini had continued to push the boundaries of what cinema could do, engulfing his audience in a world so unique and so packed with visual wonder, it was almost suffocating. A competing film also made from the Petronius tale, and also called *Satyricon,* came out around the same time. To distinguish the two, producers titled Federico's film *Fellini Satyricon.* Federico did not object. One wag commented, "Everything is about Fellini anyway; he is the real star, so why not?"

In January 1970, just weeks before Federico's fiftieth birthday, he and Giulietta went to America to begin the press tour for *Satyricon.* The American Film Institute in Los Angeles was thrilled to have him as a guest, taking questions from the head of the esteemed institute, George Stevens, and film students. Tickets were at a premium. The audience was packed with luminaries, including Billy Wilder, John Huston, Jack Lemmon, and Ray Bradbury. They were shocked to hear Federico decry the notion that improvisation played any part in his work. It was a notion that had been assumed by some. Federico corrected them by saying that making a film was a mathematical, exact, precise business.

When asked whether he watched rushes—the raw footage shot each day—Federico scoffed at the notion, countering by asking Ray Bradbury whether he read and reread what he wrote during the day. Bradbury had to admit to the audience that he did not reread everything each day; it would stunt his work. He needed to keep moving forward. Federico had made his point. He concluded the evening by saying that for him, everything that happened on and around the set—the real life that was occurring every day—was a part of each film, and that being able to absorb and to have imagination about it all was the essence of his work. He told the audience of filmmakers and students of film, "The picture is in my head. I just try to make it."

On the final leg of the press tour, in late winter of 1970, *Satyricon* was shown at 1:00 a.m. on a huge screen at Madison Square Garden in New York City after a rock concert. It was a blustery night with snowflakes beginning to fall. Painted vans, school buses with peace signs, and motorcycles ringed the entire block around the intersection of 34th Street and 7th Avenue. Federico and Giulietta were driven through the streets and arrived at the arena at midnight. They were stunned to see the spectacle of ten thousand young people. The smell of hashish and marijuana permeated the air; a gigantic cloud of haze hung over the crowd.

The film began and the crowd seemed to delight in it, applauding frequently. The atmosphere seemed as otherworldly to Federico as the one he had created onscreen. He looked at his wife. She was dressed, as always, elegantly and tastefully. Federico himself was wearing a Brioni suit. There was no denying they were of a different generation. They were two people no longer in the prime of their lives. The freedom of the American young people was so vastly different from their own youth, constricted by the tyranny of Fascism and the destruction of war. "I'd like to be young today," said Federico wistfully.

During the 1970s, television made its final assault on revolutionizing cultural life in Italy. The viewing habits changed permanently and cinemas all over Italy were feeling the loss of audiences. Some closed, never to reopen again. Federico became fascinated by the possibilities of the medium after initially decrying its effects on the viewers. After finding the experience of *A Director's Notebook* satisfying, he agreed to do another documentary. He appreciated the relative simplicity and economy of making television. But with Federico, nothing was ever simple. He agreed to make a film for television about a subject dear to his heart: clowns. He began by interviewing clowns and visiting circuses in Italy and Paris.

Federico also agreed to appear onscreen as himself in the film *Alex in Wonderland,* directed by a young American, Paul Mazursky. Mazursky was a huge fan of Federico's work and had requested a meeting with him while visiting Italy. He was persistent and they finally had lunch at Cesarina, one of Federico's haunts. Federico was charmed by the brash young American and invited him to come along while he scouted locations. They spent several days together and Mazursky worked up the courage to ask if Federico would appear in his film. Federico, who never said no directly to anyone, agreed on the spot and promptly forgot about it. When Mazursky contacted Federico's press secretary Mario Longardi to let him know that he would be coming to Italy to shoot the scene, Federico said he had reconsidered and could not do the role.

Mazursky pretended he didn't understand and flew to Rome the next day, tracking Federico down at Cesarina. Entrapped, Federico had to agree. Besides, he had to admire Mazursky's moxie. Once Federico had committed, he helped set up the location, a hallway at Cinecittà, and an editing booth, and performed the scene exactly as written, taking direction with humility. His partner in the scene was Donald Sutherland, who was in a fever of disbelief that he was actually acting on film with Federico Fellini. Mazursky and Federico remained lifelong friends. Meeting Sutherland would prove to have great consequence for Federico in the near future.

On a trip to Riccione, a town near Rimini, to visit and do research with the Orfei family circus, Federico was in an accident while driving his green Mercedes convertible. Initially he thought he had killed a young boy on a motorcycle. The image of the adolescent sprawled on the highway was terrifying. It seemed to Federico as though his entire life shattered at that moment. The sun shone on the boy's silky blond hair. The sound of the sea splashing against the side of the highway mixed with the voices of concerned motorists who stopped to see what had happened. Then, as if by a miracle, the boy rose up and shook himself off. He was slightly unsteady, but it was clear that he had not been seriously harmed. Federico felt as though two lives had been saved.

There was a German tourist in the gathered crowd who recognized Federico. He was respectful, however, given the circumstance, and refrained from addressing Federico. He was shocked, therefore, when Federico walked up to him.

"Do you see the green Mercedes?" asked Federico.

"Yes," stammered the man, who understood only a little Italian.

"Would you like to have it?" asked Federico, brandishing the keys.

The German man couldn't believe he had heard correctly, but before he could say anything, Federico grabbed his hand and put the keys in his palm.

"My wife is Giulietta Masina, as you know. It is under her name, as is everything. She will take care of you. Goodbye and good luck!"

Federico hitched a ride to Riccione with a truck driver who had no idea he had picked up the great director. They discussed the price of pigs while Federico's adrenaline readjusted. He never drove again.

He bought a bike. Friends and colleagues grew used to seeing a large figure wearing a black Stetson riding up to restaurants and appointments on a small bicycle. The taxi drivers of Rome grew familiar with him. He loved hearing their stories. The years of midnight drives to discuss ideas with collaborators were over. Now meetings took place in his apartment on via Margutta or in one of the many Roman trattorias he so loved.

Federico continued with his work on the documentary. He decided to appear in the film as himself, an interested, inquiring interviewer. The subject of clowns and circuses was the source of some of his earliest and most complex memories. He admitted he was at once enthralled and terrified by clowns and their environment, the circus. The documentary pointed out that in the clown world, there were two different types. The white clown represented authority, order, what one is "supposed to do." The "Augusto" clown was the naughty child, the rabble-rouser, the one who upends all expectations and challenges the status quo. Federico's theory was that every human being has within him both of these clowns and that our lives are in a constant dialogue between these two sides.

I Clowns, as the film was titled, has three sections. The first part is Federico's memories of the circus as a child in Rimini and the actual people in Rimini, the town characters who were themselves clownlike. The second part is made up of visits by Federico and his crew to the homes of aging clowns. One aging performer says wistfully, "You always miss the past, and your youth. The circus was my life. Now . . . I feed my canary and there's my wife . . . but I can't forget the circus." Federico leaves the house of this wistful man saying, "Damn. Old age is terrible." The last part of *I Clowns* is a funeral for a clown performed in an absurd circus ring with a reunion of the clowns who have appeared in the film. The final scene is a reconciliation between the white clown and Augusto, underscored by a haunting melody.

Delving into the hearts and souls of clowns and, by extension, the circus brought out Federico's own deep connection to the memories of his childhood as well as the passage of a performer and creative artist into old age. The film is also an indictment of the changing nature of the modern audience, whose tastes and ability to appreciate circus performers was rapidly changing.

There was confusion and strife regarding when and how *I Clowns* would be shown. But Christmas 1970 found Federico in Rimini with his mother watching *I Clowns* in black and white on her small television. Ida was now seventy-four, but had lost none of her energy or verve.

She patted Federico's face, as she might have done forty-five years before, and said, "I didn't like clowns long ago. I was afraid they would steal you away. It seems they have."

It was beginning to snow, but Ida insisted they take a walk near the sea after Christmas dinner. They could see the Grand Hotel, with its snapping flags and twinkling lights, in the distance. Ida was slightly unsteady and she held on to her son's arm.

"You won't make any more troublesome films, will you, Fefe? Maybe a nice one about here in Rimini?"

Federico gazed out to the beach and the sea beyond, which was pearl gray in the fading winter light. Several teenagers had made snowballs. They were throwing them at the backside of a shapely woman who was tottering down the boardwalk next to the sea. She wore a pair of spike heels and a large white fur coat that flapped in the wind. *We are all clowns,* he thought, *but some of us just don't know it.*

Chapter Eleven

THE DREAM OF MEMORY

Giulietta awoke with a start. Her typewriter had slipped off the bed. Books and papers were strewn about. The window that looked out on via Margutta was open. It was pouring rain and windy. The shutters were banging against the outside walls of the apartment. She realized she had fallen asleep while working on her advice column for the newspaper. She remembered the last thing she had read: an angry letter from a feminist who had seen an early marketing poster for Federico's new film, *Roma*. Because it depicted a woman on all fours with three dangling breasts, feminists were apparently outraged. Federico's old friend Rinaldo Geleng had designed it along with his sons. Giulietta had to agree that the design could be seen as offensive. On the other hand, it was supposed to be reminiscent of the she-wolf who founded Rome.

Giulietta closed the window against the rain. Now she could hear Federico on the phone in the next room. At the stroke of seven o'clock every morning now, it seemed, he was on the phone. People lauded her husband. The invitations, awards, and accolades piled up. But the one thing he needed, money, was not so easy to find.

Giulietta had proposed a potential producer for *Roma*. He was Turi Vasile, an old friend from her theater days at the university. He had now become a film producer and was eager to work with directors of stature. Many producers in Europe and America in the early 1970s were wary of Federico's reputation for going over budget. They were also aware of his reputation for creating cinema magic and for pushing the boundaries of what cinema could do.

Vasile found the money, in partnership with an American company, and Federico and his co-writer, Bernardino Zapponi, had begun their research. They wrote a script that began with a young boy's desire to escape the confines and provinciality of his small town and go to Rome. Arriving in Rome, he experiences the characters in his boardinghouse, a boisterous though warm street celebration, sexual initiation at various brothels. Then the film moves forward to present-day Rome: the tourists, the counterculture movement as contrasted with the humanity and fun of a vaudeville theater from the past. The story moves on to an exploration of a subterranean tunnel and the discovery of a beautiful preserved ancient Roman household. The magical moment is ruined when the fetid air from present-day Rome seeps in and ruins the frescoes. There is an ecclesiastical fashion show replete with an ever more ludicrous parade of religious icons.

The final scene of *Roma* takes place on the Grande Raccordo Anulare, the forty-two-mile, ring-shaped orbital motorway that encircles Rome. It was built as a way to route the ever-increasing car and truck traffic around the city just after World War II. Completed in 1970, the road became for Federico a symbol of the current Rome and the brutalization of the city by the constant and apocryphal presence of loud, pollution-spewing cars and motorcycles. During the scene in the film, phalanxes of motorcycles buzz round and round the city, passing by, and ignoring, its ancient monuments, oblivious to their history or meaning.

Federico filmed much of *Roma* on Stage 2 at Cinecittà, where designer Danilo Donati had built a portion of the Grande Raccordo Anulare, an entire city block to replicate via Albalonga, and a set to represent a sixteenth-century mansion for the ecclesiastical fashion show. When Federico had completed shooting three-fourths of the film, the Swiss bank that was financing the film went under. Production had to be shut down completely while financing was found.

One of the scenes yet to be shot, and most important to Federico, was one in which he goes to Anna Magnani's apartment for an interview. For Federico, *Roma* represented a look at the city that had created and nurtured him as an artist. What better symbol of the earthiness, the raw passion, the strength and resilience that was Rome than the beloved actress Anna Magnani? Yet in the film, when Federico suggests to her, at her front door, that she is the perfect symbol of Rome, she scoffs at the notion. In a film replete with Roman symbols, religious, sexual, and historic, Magnani refuses to be reduced to a symbol; she is flesh and blood. She closes the door on Federico, saying, "Federico, get some sleep. I don't trust you."

It was her final appearance on film. Magnani died in September 1973. Although the romantic relationship she had with Roberto Rossellini was long over, Rossellini honored their artistic friendship by burying her in the Rossellini family mausoleum. The humanity she brought to her work had deeply affected Federico as a young artist. The death of Magnani reminded him more than ever of the importance of the events of his youth. He had begun to explore it, in various sequences in his films, for years. He now felt ready to explore the ghosts of his past and put them to rest.

The response to *Fellini's Roma* was tepid and at times negative. Romans expecting to see a paean to their city were shocked and disappointed to see venality, greed, and non-romanticized brothels alongside the cacophony and disruption of modern life. The juxtaposition of the past with the present, which some found confusing, was exactly Federico's point: We can't escape our history; our past shapes us and sometimes controls us if we can't find freedom in understanding.

On May 6, 1974, Titta Benzi, Federico's boyhood friend, walked out of the cinema in Rimini with tears streaming down his face. Now a lawyer, Titta had just seen the new film Federico had made. Titta had watched it three times in succession, along with other denizens of Rimini. They had seen snippets of their town in *I Vitelloni*, *8½*, and *Fellini's Roma*. The life of their famous friend Federico had been refracted through his unique imagination in many forms on film. But *Amarcord*, or "I remember" in

Romagnolo dialect, was the film that was most directly related to the Rimini they knew in the mid-1930s.

Many of the people depicted in the film had died or moved away, although Federico's mother, Ida, and sister, Maddalena, and her family still lived in Rimini. Rimini itself was bombed over two hundred times during World War II and much of it had been rebuilt. Significantly, Federico had rebuilt the piazzas, fountains, passageways, shops, and even the Fulgor cinema at Cinecittà. A hotel that resembled the Grand Hotel in Anzio was used for that location. The sea at Ostia was used for ocean scenes. Federico did not want to film in or near Rimini for many reasons, the chief one being that he wished to avoid "advice" from the Riminese. The idea for making a film about adolescence in Rimini had been a part of Federico's creative conscience for years. His manner of looking at history, at the facts of lives, had been honed during *Satyricon, I Clowns,* and *Roma.* It was almost as if this "enhanced memory" was the final step, an inevitable film. Because so much of what happens in the film is filtered through Federico's own unique memory, he did not solicit or want input from the people with whom he had grown up.

Amarcord doesn't explore the family in which Federico was raised. Instead, the "adopted" family of Titta Benzi is the focal point of the story. The gregarious, eccentric Benzi family offers a panoply of characters: the Fascist-hating father, the lazy good-for-nothing uncle, the doting mother, and, of course, Titta himself. Through the core of this family and their adolescent son coming of age, Federico takes a look at the extinction of reality caused by living under Fascist rule and the smothering, infantilizing result of a political time in which the populace is told what to do, what to believe, and how to live. The specter of Mussolini appears and reappears, sometimes in comedic ways. But underneath the comedy of life in a small town in Italy in the 1930s, there is always something sinister in the background.

The adolescent boy, played by Venetian newcomer Bruno Zanin, spends the film doing what adolescent boys do. He tries to break free, to explore new religious, sexual, and moral pathways in the small village. He tries to individuate, but is always caught up short by the limitations of his education, age, religion, and, most of all, the repression of the Fascist world in which he lives. Gradisca, the shapely beautician who is the focus of all of Titta's fantasies, represents the ultimate in feminine beauty and power.

Federico begged his friend, actress Sandra Milo, to play the part. He went to her home in person to do a screen test. When the test ended and Federico was about to depart, he had a strange feeling. He felt that the actress, who had worked with him so often and so memorably, would not do the role. Her jealous husband refused to allow her to work in a film, particularly one directed by Fellini. Federico's intuition was right and Milo turned down the chance to play Gradisca. He sent her one hundred red roses and a note expressing his disappointment. Magali Noël, who had played Fortunata in *Satyricon,* was more than happy to take the role.

Federico chose a new writer, Tonino Guerra, with whom to work on *Amarcord.* Guerra was exactly Federico's age and had grown up in a small town five miles from Rimini. Guerra had been sent to a German labor camp during the war and there he became a poet. He was also a respected screenwriter who had worked on many films with directors such as Antonioni. Unlike Federico, Guerra loved his small town and his boyhood home and spent long stretches of time there. The two men spoke the same dialect. They knew the small-town mannerisms and ways of behaving. They instinctively understood the mien and rhythm of lives spent in a provincial place under the yoke of Fascism. They knew the humor and pathos that came from presenting the people they knew so well without judgment or moralizing. It was an easy collaboration.

The film is episodic. It takes place during the time span of a year in the mid-thirties, from a fall festival to a spring wedding. Federico had to dodge endless questions from journalists and townspeople, all of whom wanted to "put in their two cents" about what should be in the film. Instead, he made his personal memories according to his ideas and life experience. Jungian symbols abound: the bonfire at the start of the film; the magical passing of the SS *Rex,* the most powerful ocean liner of its time; the gray waves of the sea; the landing of the peacock, the ultimate symbol of death, during a snowstorm; the beauty and hope of a wedding. *Amarcord* embraces the life cycle of a year. As a poignant analysis of what happens under Fascist rule, it highlights the resilience, humor, and human urges of a populace that refuses to give up its individuality and sense of joy in life.

Audiences immediately loved *Amarcord,* as did most critics. It was a box office hit, the first one Federico had experienced in over ten years. *Amarcord* would prove to be the final film of Federico's that had wide distribution and success at the box office. At the age of fifty-four, Federico was done with exploring the past and adolescence.

Or so he thought. A few years earlier, in 1971, on a whim, he had signed a simple but binding contract with his old friend and sometimes-enemy Dino De Laurentiis. The contract specified a film based on the life of Casanova.

Amarcord had a warm, elegiac quality; the adolescent yearnings of the main character were relatable and universal. Federico's next project plumbed the depth of an infamously cold, calculating, predatory human being whose life was supposedly detailed in a literary work from the eighteenth century. It had captivated readers for centuries and was based on the life of Giacomo Casanova. Born in 1725 to parents who were actors, Casanova became a lawyer, then was jailed for insubordination. He traveled throughout Europe, supposedly becoming a card shark, ladies' man, medium, and financier. He died in 1798 after having written a memoir about his exploits with women. As a certain symbol of Latin manhood, the word "Casanova" came to denote power, disdain for convention, and exotic consumption without regard for consequence.

Although Federico, in a weak moment, had signed that contract to make the movie with De Laurentiis, when he actually read the memoir, he was so disgusted by Casanova that he tore pages out of the book. He stated on many occasions that he despised the character and felt Casanova lived in a state of perpetual adolescence.

Universal Pictures, eager to cash in on the Fellini name and the success of *Amarcord,* agreed to co-finance the film. They were particularly excited when Federico brought his expat friend Gore Vidal along to co-write the screenplay. Vidal maintained an elegant residence in Rome and the two had been friends for years. Vidal nicknamed Federico "Freddie" and Federico paid back the favor by calling Vidal "Gorino." The two worked together on an English version of a screenplay about Casanova, but Vidal had one sticking point: Federico seemed to hate the character. How could he expect the audience to invest in such a despicable person? Would they not hate him as well? Vidal was soon released from the project.

Casting began for the leading role. American icons Marlon Brando, Al Pacino, and Robert Redford were all vetoed by Federico and soon De Laurentiis began to have cold feet. When he backed out of the project, Andrea Rizzoli, the son of producer Angelo Rizzoli, came forward. Eventually Rizzoli, too, backed out as the budget began to balloon. The film ended up being produced by Alberto Grimaldi, who shut down the production at one point on December 23, 1975, due to union issues and cost overruns.

Federico had finally found the actor to play Casanova. He was Donald Sutherland, with whom Federico had shared the screen years earlier in a scene from Paul Mazursky's film *Alex in Wonderland.* A tall, lanky Canadian actor with twenty years of experience in film, Sutherland had worked successfully with high-profile directors like Robert Aldrich, Robert Altman, and John Schlesinger. He was a consummate professional and deeply intellectual. He came to the role impeccably prepared, having read and studied the memoir, the time period, the historical context. He was ready to discuss character nuance with the great maestro.

To say the least, this was not the way in which Federico worked. The film was deep inside of him, as Sutherland came to feel, as if he were trying to remember something in his mind and get the actor to do it. It was as if he were a sort of conductor attempting to conjure music out of an actor. Sutherland felt that he was in the presence of a genius, someone who was inviting all who worked with him on a magical journey of creativity and freedom. This is not to say that it was easy for Sutherland or anyone else working with Federico. The director had developed a way of working, over the years, in which he expected the cast and crew to simply enter into the life he created on set. They had to intuit what to do, sometimes without a script.

Federico was obsessed with Casanova's appearance and Sutherland routinely spent three hours a day in the makeup chair. His eyebrows were shaved off and raised. His hairline was shaved off and set back. He had a fake nose and chin. Ever the professional, Sutherland remained open to the process, thoroughly committed and prepared, on time to the set and ready to execute whatever direction he could get. It was almost as if Federico took out his dislike of the character on the actor. Sutherland remained calm and focused to the end.

After the final shot, director and actor hugged. Federico presented him with a watch as a gift. Sutherland walked off the set, stumbling as he removed his incredibly heavy wardrobe coat.

He returned to his dressing room, which Federico had outfitted in authentic eighteenth-century furniture in addition to a continual supply of chocolate elixir, Casanova's favorite drink. He looked at the card, signed by Federico, that came with the watch. It said: *Dreams are the only reality.*

Visits to the set of *Casanova* were a daily occurrence. Journalists, celebrities, and students of film were welcomed by Federico, partly because he liked to have the life on set, but also because it provided free marketing for the film itself. One young director who was recommended to Federico by his friend Paul Mazursky came to the set and impressed Federico with his volley of questions, his curiosity, and his obvious knowledge of filmmaking. He was very young. He took a lot of pictures. His name was Steven Spielberg.

Casanova was a film reviled by critics and unpopular at the box office. It seemed that Gore Vidal's prediction about the despicable aspect of the lead character had come true. With *Amarcord* and *Casanova,* one about adolescence and the other about a man who never grew out of adolescence, Federico had experienced great success and questionable failure. He was ready, at the age of fifty-five, to leave adolescence behind.

On April 4, 1975, he won his fourth Academy Award, for *Amarcord.* Deeply involved in work on *Casanova* and sure he would not win, Federico did not attend. He believed now that his cinema was more like painting—it was essence, style, ideology, light. It was these elements he wanted to explore. If he could only find someone who wanted to pay for it.

Giulietta and Federico were at Mario Romagnoli's restaurant

when the good news came. It was breakfast time in Rome and the place became filled with paparazzi and well-wishers. Federico looked over the festive crowd and wondered who among them might want to finance his next film.

Chapter Twelve

THE DREAM OF CHAOS

Federico had finally secured a producer for *City of Women,* the next feature film he wanted to make. The man was none other than Renzo Rossellini, the son of his former mentor, Roberto Rossellini. The film was to be a tribute to the power and strength of women, and the producer hoped it would be Federico's response to the criticism of his films by feminists.

On March 16, 1976, Federico had taken Giulietta to lunch at one of his favorite restaurants to celebrate the signing of the contracts for *City of Women.* They were at Hosteria Romana, a restaurant at the corner of via Rasella and via del Boccaccio, not far from the Trevi Fountain. Federico loved to tempt Giulietta, who was always watching her weight, with the creamy carbonara that was a specialty of the house. Gigi Fazzi, the gregarious owner, adored Federico, kept a special corner table for him, and plied him with concoctions made especially for him, knowing Federico's love of cooking from Emilia-Romagna. Federico turned nothing away. His style of eating was to sample a little bit of everything, even if it came from someone else's plate.

They were digging into an antipasto of San Daniele ham when Fazzi appeared at their table. He was wringing his hands. Rivers of sweat poured down his wide forehead. He dabbed at them with thick kitchen towels.

"It's Moro. Aldo Moro," he said.

Federico and Giulietta looked up. They had been deep in conversation about casting for *City of Women*. They had agreed on the lead; no one but Marcello Mastroianni would do.

"Yes, I know him . . . ," said Federico about Moro, tilting his head.

There seemed to be more that Fazzi had to say. He didn't seem to want to say it.

"He has been kidnapped," he blurted out. "Your friend—kidnapped. By the Red Brigade. They killed five of his bodyguards in a shootout in via Fani. I am so, so sorry. I am sorry for your friend. Sorry for Italy. For Rome. Sorry for ruining your beautiful lunch, your beautiful day."

Federico and Giulietta were deeply shocked, as was the entire country. The Red Brigades was a far-left terrorist organization founded in 1970, although it had roots in the partisans formed during World War II. Known for kidnappings, murders, and sabotage, including "knee-capping"—shooting a person in the knees so they would be handicapped for life—their primary goal was to undermine the Italian state and to pave the way for a Marxist upheaval. As the president of the Christian Democratic party, Aldo Moro represented everything they wanted to destroy.

The turmoil and agony over the kidnapping was a part of every conversation, and even more so because Federico knew him personally. Federico was immediately drawn to the idea of creating a film for television that would express the confusion, fear, and uncertainty these acts of violence and aggression had aroused. The discovery fifty-five days later of Moro's body in the trunk of a car, on via Caetana near the Communist Party headquarters, did nothing to quell the sense of disorder and fear among the populace. It was a gruesome capstone to the increasing sense of unease and lack of trust in the government.

Although Federico often claimed that he was apolitical, it was nearly impossible to ignore the gathering sense of doom and destruction that was rampant in the political life of his city and country. He sought a way to express this brewing storm.

Federico had long been fascinated by orchestras, though he was by no means a fan of music. He had little interest in listening to it unless it was a score for one of his films written by Nino Rota. He was intrigued by human nature. He often said that he was less interested in what happened onscreen in films—for example, in the love affairs, the storylines, the characters—than he was in the actual audience sitting with him in the theater. He loved to watch the lovers sitting in front of him, the hat-check girls gossiping, the candy seller yawning. Similarly, he was much more interested in exploring the human behavior and motivation of the musicians in orchestras than in listening to the music they produced. For years, Federico had been awed by the fact that so many disparate people could come together for a recording session with Rota, and within minutes sit down and begin to play an entire score with unity and grace.

Federico began to work on an outline for a film that would center on an orchestra rehearsal. He brought on his friend Brunello Rondi as a co-writer. The script began to shape itself into a story about an orchestra that comes together to rehearse in an ancient sacristy. They are interviewed individually about their various instruments and their relationship to their work. They gossip among themselves, flirt, discuss health problems and union meetings. There are strange rumblings outside the building. The maestro arrives and brutalizes the musicians, berating them for their lack of passion, petty concerns, and lack of coherence. He becomes livid and stomps away at a break. The musicians rebel, spray-painting revolutionary sentiments on the walls, throwing things at the podium, destroying the room, and fighting with one another. The building itself begins to disintegrate. Dust and destruction rain down. The maestro picks up his baton once more. The orchestra, standing as their chairs have been crushed, now plays together as one. Despite this, the maestro begins to correct, berate, and demand perfection.

Federico spent a month of research interviewing members of a real orchestra one by one, with Liliane Betti taking careful notes. He invited them to meals at his beloved Cesarina restaurant, treating them to delights such as *zuppa pavese* (bread and egg soup). He found out about their reasons for playing, how they felt about their lives, how they felt about various conductors. A producer, Leonardo Pescarolo, came on board. He knew Federico's reputation concerning budgets and production schedules and was wary of taking the risk to work with the great director. Federico, acutely aware of this fear, seemed determined to prove him wrong. He set about directing a film that would come in on time and under budget. Danilo Donati created a set in one large space, making an ancient sacristy—a religious underworld lit in a manner that seemed halfway between color and black and white. The cast of unknowns was hired not for their musical ability, but for the uniqueness of their faces. They were taught to play well enough for their roles in the film.

Federico shot the film in four short weeks. He remained on schedule and within his budget.

Orchestra Rehearsal starts with the cacophony of traffic noise and ambulance sirens over the opening credits. The rehearsal in the film begins in a seemingly calm manner: Musicians arrive and set up for their day, tuning their instruments, listening to soccer matches, positioning their music stands, and claiming their space. It ultimately dissolves into chaos and destruction. The musicians rebel against their conductor, which results in the disintegration of what they are trying to achieve: a unity of sound and purpose. In the end, says one character, "Each of us must focus on our own instrument. It is all we can do." The final words of the film are spoken by the conductor to the orchestra: "*Da capo!*"—which, in musical terms, means to play from the beginning. Despite whatever tragedy life brings, that is all any of us can do—figure out a way to begin again.

The film premiered in May 1978 at an establishment gala held at the Palazzo del Quirinale, the presidential palace in Rome. It was attended by members of the government who all had different interpretations of its meaning. Clearly it was a metaphor for a cataclysmic moment in the history of their country, when terrorism was flourishing and the seed for what had caused the disenfranchisement of youth and the working classes had yet to be addressed. It seemed to ask the eternal question of what happens when a society has lost faith in its leaders. Federico, as always, refused to take sides. He felt his work should speak for itself.

On the evening of April 9, 1979, Federico and his friend Nino Rota had dinner at Cesarina and walked together to the gallery opening of a mutual friend, Fabrizio Clerici. After the opening, they walked along the Tiber River, discussing the fantastical world Clerici depicted in his work. They shared their admiration for the worlds he created. They were nearing via Margutta. The narrow street was filled with flower boxes that were just beginning to blossom. Federico picked up one of the delicate petals.

"I sometimes wish I had been a painter," sighed Federico.

"You are a painter, Fefe. Your subjects move. And speak," said Rota.

He tipped his hat to his friend Federico and walked down via Margutta. Rota was whistling a tune, a new tune that Federico suspected would be a part of the new film *City of Women.* Federico picked up the melody and hummed it as he walked up the steps of his apartment.

The next day he was at Cinecittà overseeing preparations for the start of *City of Women* when Liliane Betti came to him. She was crying.

"Nino. He's gone," she said in her simple, straightforward manner.

Rota had died the night before, in his sleep, of a heart attack.

The loss of his artistic muse and friend was almost unbearable for Federico. Nino Rota, Federico knew, was as responsible as anyone for the profoundly emotional aspects of so much of his work. The ineffable sense of loneliness and human tragedy as well as joy that can come at a moment's notice—these were the qualities that his music evoked. Although the results were never complicated or pretentious, Rota's scores were built on the genius complexities of a brilliant artist and his intrinsic understanding of the creative mind of his friend Federico.

Giulietta, too, was devastated and could not stop crying at the service in Sant'Agostino Church. She returned to via Margutta as soon as the service concluded.

Suso Cecchi d'Amico, a woman who was a renowned screenwriter and friend to both Rota and Federico, asked for a moment of Federico's time. They walked to the Piazza Navona and sat on a bench. It was a beautiful April day and the splash of the Trevi Fountain obscured their conversation from the crowds of tourists who flocked there.

"I need to tell you a story," she said. "I am asking you for a favor. I need for you to come with me to see Nino's family. I can't do this alone. I have to tell them something shocking." She paused briefly before continuing. "Nino has a secret daughter. She is nearly an adult. She is the result of a relationship he had long ago with a fellow music student. He has been supporting her throughout her life, sometimes with my help, asking me to take her money and so forth."

In a state of shock, Federico complied with his friend's request and accompanied her. He was impressed by the care and kindness with which she revealed the secret to the Rota family. He was even more surprised, and a little hurt, that through all the years, all the late nights, all the drives around Rome, all the recording sessions, the hundreds of hours they had spent together, Rota had never spoken a word about his daughter.

"We can never really know another person, can we?" he said to Giulietta that evening.

She was cutting him a slice of *erbazzone,* a savory pie made of chard and pancetta. Giulietta had made it for him because she knew he loved it and it would comfort him. She placed the slice on a china plate and put it in front of him.

"No, Fefe. We can't ever really know another person. But we keep trying, don't we?" She took a tiny bite of the buttery crust. "That's the flavor of life."

"The great ones make things simple, don't they? Joyful. As soon as he entered the room, everything turned festive, fantastic," Federico said. "He made everything come alive."

The loss of Nino Rota left a great emptiness that could not be filled. Other talented composers were hired, but they never had the same effect on Federico's filmmaking process. Rota was effortlessly understanding of Federico's unique artistry.

City of Women was plagued by a series of tragedies and disasters, as well as timing. One of the important aspects of the changing world of the 1970s was the feminist movement in Italy. *City of Women* was, in part, Federico's response to the changes he saw and felt in Italian society. It examines one man's response to the idea of the female. In Federico's mind, it was a dream and at times a nightmare of a man who finds himself in the midst of a feminist convention.

The production was difficult. It was the third film of Federico's in which Marcello Mastroianni had starred. The two men worked in an almost wordless simpatico, as though they were mirrors of one another. The same could not be said for Ettore Manni, a seasoned older actor with a drinking problem. Although Federico was known throughout the world as an iconoclast and a rule breaker, that did not apply to behavior on the set. He demanded, and usually got, complete focus and absolute dedication to the work at hand from everyone involved with production. After his experience working on *Il Bidone,* in which he had to deal daily with Broderick Crawford's alcoholism, he had no patience for actors who came to work inebriated.

In addition to his irresponsible behavior, Manni had a habit of bringing a loaded gun to the set. He and Manni had screaming fights that usually ended with Manni stalking off the set. One day, after a particularly brutal argument, Federico actually stopped the shoot for the day, something that never happened on a Fellini set. The next day, on July 27, 1979, Manni was found in his hotel room, dead from a gunshot wound. It was never determined whether it was an accident or suicide.

The film was not well received by critics and did little to quell feminist criticism of Federico's films.

As the 1970s came to an end, Federico had to acknowledge that the world he had known had changed culturally and politically. The Rome he had fallen in love with was responding to a generation that no longer went as often to the cinema. They questioned authority and demanded social change. The coming decade would challenge Federico to keep creating in a world that revered him as an artist but that increasingly denied him the opportunity to create art.

Chapter Thirteen

THE DREAM OF THE FUTURE

Giulietta had done a television series, *Camilla,* in 1976 and the episodes reran frequently on Italian television. All of Italy seemed thrilled to have her back in their living rooms. She allowed herself only one pastry a week and today was the day. It was late October, 1983. The sun was out and she and Federico decided to take advantage of one of the last warm days to have their breakfast outside, under the striped awning of the Caffè Greco. The azure sky of Rome made them cheerful. The waiter, who knew them well, brought them two *cornetti.*

"I know Federico claims to not want one and then eats half of yours," he said with a wink.

As he did so, three young girls came to the table. They were German tourists and they were shy and respectful. They all held autograph books. For a moment, Federico wondered whether their parents might have occupied Rome forty years ago. He had picked up his *cornetto,* but he put it down, wiped his hands on a napkin, and prepared to be gracious, sign autographs, and even answer questions if he could understand what they were saying.

But they ignored him and turned, in unison, toward Giulietta. She lowered her sunglasses and peered at them over the top. She had not worn eye makeup and she felt self-conscious.

"Oh, Miss Masina. We have all seen you on television. We all want to be actresses like you. Would you sign our books? We've brought a present, hoping that maybe we would see you."

One of the girls produced a beautiful silk scarf wrapped in tissue.

"A beautiful scarf. For our idol," the girl said.

Giulietta removed her sunglasses and wiped away tears. She carefully signed each book.

"But I really can't accept the scarf, sweethearts. It is just too much."

"No. No. You must. We all want to be actresses. Like you. Tell us what to do. Do you have any advice?"

"Find a genius director who creates for you the roles of a lifetime," she answered, looking at Federico. She couldn't tell if he was amused or annoyed.

The girls began to walk away and Giulietta called after them, "And never, ever give up hope!"

As they walked home that day, Giulietta was intensely grateful that in two short weeks Federico would begin shooting *And the Ship Sails On.*

On November 11, 1983, Federico did indeed step onto the soundstage of Cinecittà and prepare for his first shot of *And the Ship Sails On.* Nine soundstages had been converted into separate parts of the luxury ocean liner on which the whole film took place. Since Federico was not content to film on or near the ocean, one was created by stagehands who rippled gigantic sheets of cellophane. White puffs of smoke against a huge scrim created the clouds in the sky. When one actress commented there weren't enough stars in the sky, Federico reached up and punched some holes in the scrim. Pins of light seeped through. Now there were stars. The idea of making a film about a group of artists sailing out to sea to scatter the ashes of a great opera singer appealed to him.

It had been two and a half years since Federico had stepped onto a soundstage. They had been years full of frustration. Federico found a grand irony in the fact that he was lauded around the world as a master of cinematic art yet could not find financing to make a film. Projects had come and gone. The apartment on via Margutta was now filled to the brim with awards and trophies. Yet Federico spent sleepless nights, always a victim of insomnia, waiting until it was 7:00 a.m. and he could begin his round of phone calls to potential producers, pitching projects that never came to fruition. Ironically, journalists, fans, celebrities, and students begged him to read their screenplays and treatments, to give talks, to answer questions, to hire them. They wanted to be near the Fellini magic, but no one seemed to want to finance what had brought him fame in the first place. Federico hated and feared the idleness that descended, the mind-numbing round of insistent admirers who wanted to bask in what they called his genius.

There were detractors, too, who criticized Federico and claimed he was overrated. His most fierce defender and still his muse, his stability in life, was Giulietta. They had maintained a marriage through forty years, through the vicissitudes of international fame and the triumphs and pressures of public life. They were forever connected by mutual respect and not a little competition; they often argued fiercely among themselves. But they were fiercely loyal to one another regarding their work as artists.

Drawn to the idea of a period piece, perhaps because of the success of *Amarcord,* and financed partly by RAI (Italian state television), Federico and screenwriter Tonino Guerra began to imagine a film that would be based on the story they had heard about Maria Callas's ashes being spread over the Aegean Sea. Federico traveled to Genoa to inspect the SS *Guglielmo Marconi,* a luxury ship he would use for inspiration for the set of *And the Ship Sails On.*

Federico broke with his longstanding habit of going through piles of photographs and hiring professional as well as non-professional actors. He went instead to London and held more traditional auditions. He wanted to hire actors with a sense of rigor and professional training. The British actors did not disappoint. They came to auditions prepared, chatted for a moment about the weather, and got down to business. They didn't analyze the script, argue about interpretation, or discuss deals. If he asked them to stand on their head, they did. There was no wheedling or pouting.

He hired Freddie Jones and Norma West, two revered British character actors, as well as Pina Bausch, the renowned choreographer and director of the German company Tanztheater Wuppertal. When Norma West arrived in Italy, she was carrying what she called her "lucky teddy bear." Federico remembered this and invited her to bring it to the set to make her feel more at home. He noticed everything and forgot nothing.

When the film was released, there was endless marketing in the hopes that it would be a smash hit like *Amarcord*. Nevertheless, the film didn't do as well at the box office. It seemed that the general public loved Federico the man, but not always the art he created. Rimini declared the opening day of the film "Fellini Day." There were parades and celebrations, culminating at the Grand Hotel. It was bedecked with lights like the SS *Rex* in *Amarcord*. At Titta Benzi's urging, the city bought their famous son a house at the beach and presented it to him with much fanfare. It was a lovely gesture, but when Giulietta and Federico attempted to occupy the house, they discovered there were many liens against it; the people of Rimini had only put down a deposit on it. The saying went that Fellini may have made *Il Bidone* ("The Con"), but Rimini conned Fellini. Giulietta and Federico remained permanently in Rome in their apartment on via Margutta.

Federico, who had maintained a vital interest in the occult and mysticism, was amazed by the work of Carlos Castaneda. Castaneda's book *The Teachings of Don Juan* described his meetings with esoteric parapsychological master Don Juan Matus. Federico wanted to meet Castaneda and contacted his publisher in New York, who claimed that a young boy delivered the manuscripts to the company; they had no idea how to contact Castaneda. A psychic in Rome finally put Federico in touch with the man. Though Federico hated traveling, he went to Los Angeles to meet Castaneda and to convince him to let

Federico make a film based on his writing. He was shocked to find not a guru, but an average man dressed in pants and a button-down shirt, charming and intelligent. Castaneda invited Federico to go on an expedition to the ancient Mexican ruin of Tulum. Then Castaneda disappeared completely. Federico never heard from him again.

In September 1985, Ida Fellini died in Rimini after a long illness. The woman who had now been in Federico's life the longest, Giulietta, suggested an idea for an episode of television. It quickly and happily developed into a TV movie, the first project that husband and wife had done together in over a decade. *Ginger and Fred,* the story of two aging vaudevillians called to compete on a television game show, was an opportunity for poignance as well as for skewering the television industry and its tawdry game shows. In the film, the nostalgia of their reunion is overwhelmed by the glaring, tasteless drone of commercialism.

Marcello Mastroianni was hired to play Fred and was his usual self, light and intuitive. He was more than willing to be "aged" by makeup artists, taking on the appearance of a down-at-his-heels old vaudevillian. Giulietta, playing Ginger, was not so easy. She hated the way she looked on camera and insisted that a new cinematographer be hired. Layers of gauze were placed over the camera lens to make her wrinkles disappear.

On the final day of shooting, the scene in which Ginger and Fred dance clumsily and stumble was saved for last. As Federico and Giulietta drove to the studio that morning, it was business as usual for him; he was on the phone, cajoling and wheedling. When they got to the studio, Giulietta went to the makeup room. Federico was in and out of the room, changing a curl here and there, arching her eyebrows, making the lipstick just so. When Giulietta was ready, she walked quietly to the set. Federico was there, too, arranging the fold of a curtain, joking with the extras, adjusting the camera angle. Mastroianni arrived, half awake, as usual, even though it was noon. He had always been a night owl. They rehearsed the scene with the stumble, and then they shot it.

Then Giulietta turned to Federico. "Fefe, can we do it one last time? One last take in which we do it perfectly?"

There was a long hesitation.

"Yes, love. Do one last take. Perfectly," said Federico.

Mastroianni and Giulietta danced together, two artists who had known one another for forty years. Federico couldn't resist giving them direction. "Swoop. Twirl. Yes. Yes. That's it. That's perfection." His hands and arms followed their graceful moves with his own circles in the air. At the end of the dance, Mastroianni bowed to Giulietta. She thought she saw a tear in his eye.

"Now that we have created perfection, I need a cigarette, don't you?" Mastroianni said.

Federico was still looking through the camera lens. He had not yet said "Cut." It was as if he wanted Giulietta and Mastroianni to keep dancing forever. Then the moment passed.

"And a coffee," said Federico. "We could all use a coffee."

Federico's penultimate film was *Intervista,* a faux documentary that uses the device of the interview to celebrate Federico's beginnings as a young director at Cinecittà. It coincided with the fiftieth anniversary of the founding of the studio. The film includes a nostalgic reunion in which Mastroianni and Federico pay a visit to Anita Ekberg at her suburban home.

Voice of the Moon was Federico's final film, a parable about the whisperings of our deepest desires and dreams. It explores some of the earliest memories of Federico's beloved grandmother, Francesca, and the beauty of the life in Gambettola. With stars Roberto Benigni and Paolo Villaggio as the two sides of every human—the dignified and the anarchist—it was Federico's last critique of the loud, consumer-oriented, postmodern culture in which human beings are disconnected from the natural world: the sun, the moon, the fields of memory like Federico experienced in Gambettola. The final questions of the film are "What am I doing here? Why was I put here in the first place?" And they are answered by the last thing we hear: "If we all quieted down a little, maybe we'd understand something."

On the night of March 29, 1993, Federico walked onstage at the Academy Awards ceremony in Los Angeles. He was receiving a lifetime achievement award. His colleagues and fellow artists Sophia Loren and Marcello Mastroianni stood to receive him. Federico waved off the standing ovation and encouraged the audience to "sit down, be comfortable." He walked slowly, as he was in delicate health. He told the American audience that for him, as a young man in Italy, America and films were synonymous. Then, acknowledging the fact that he couldn't possibly thank everyone by name, he said there was only one person to really thank: Giulietta Masina. The camera panned to Giulietta, who had tears streaming down her face. Federico saw her and said, "Don't cry, Giulietta." Her face was so full of love at that moment; she became Cabiria, looking hopefully and lovingly to the future. The connection between the two, the magic of their mutual artistry, was palpable and real. To Giulietta in private, later, Federico said, "Perhaps this will lead to some work."

After suffering a heart attack at the Grand Hotel in Rimini while visiting his sister on August 3, 1993, Federico was paralyzed on the left side of his body. He requested to be moved back to Rome. Giulietta's hospital visits could barely hide her own ill health. She came every day and stayed until visiting hours were over.

October 29, 1993, was the day before their fiftieth anniversary. Giulietta wore a stylish white dress and a white turban to hide her hair loss. It pained her to see her Fefe lying in bed with tubes coming out of his arms, his hair uncombed. He was always so vain about his hair. Now it formed a wreath of white around his face and his inquisitive brown eyes.

"I've brought you the paints and pencils and brushes you asked for," she said, brandishing a large bag. "I am allowing Rinaldo Geleng to bring you an easel. But no other visitors. Even Titta. And, of course, paper, lots of paper."

"You look beautiful, as always," he said, gazing at Giulietta, "tired, but beautiful. You have no eyelashes, no eyebrows. I know what those doctors are doing to you."

Giulietta knew she couldn't fool Federico. "You are right. There is a war going on inside of me, but they say that I can win. The chemotherapy has taken my hair, so . . . less money to those ridiculous salons."

"You don't need any of that anyway. You never did. From the first time I saw you . . . pure and shining."

Giulietta took his hand. It had once been so strong and expressive. Now, as she held it, she could feel it shaking. She could see the veins in his skin.

"It was going to be a surprise," he said. "But tomorrow, on our special day, on our fiftieth, I am getting out of here. I am taking you to Cesarina's. I know, I know," he said, indicating the tubes, the room, the table of medicine, "it doesn't look promising, but one can always dream."

"Remember our first lunch?" said Giulietta. "I was so afraid you were spending too much money."

"Well, that never changed, did it?" said Federico.

They laughed. He reached for one of the drawing pads. He winced in pain and fell back on the pillow. Giulietta picked up the pad and held it for Federico. She placed six colored pencils by his side. He began to sketch. The effort exhausted him, and when he was finished, he lay back on his pillow with his eyes closed.

Giulietta gazed at the drawing. It was two clowns. One was tall with big round eyes and a shock of black hair. The other was tiny and wore a bow tie with polka dots. The taller clown was indicating that the short clown should take a bow. He was tipping his top hat to her. She winked at the audience as though she had a naughty secret. They were bathed in a shaft of golden light.

Federico died the next day, October 30, 1993. His death

made headlines around the world. Over 70,000 mourners—taxi drivers, cooks, construction workers, grips, electricians, plumbers, waitresses, caffè owners, royalty, representatives from the Vatican, hotel maids, the prime minister, princes and princesses, the famous and the infamous—filed past his casket, which was placed in the middle of Stage 5 at Cinecittà to pay homage to this man of Rome and child of Italy. In his art, they saw their dreams, their hopes, and a kind of unique soul that could only have come from their streets, their past, and their future. Giulietta Masina, his muse, joined him five months later in what can only be imagined as an artist's paradise. Fellini's physical presence had left the earth. But in his art, all of humanity has an enduring reminder to feel more whole, to explore the heights of abandon and the depths of despair, and in so doing, to be more fully alive, to embrace their dreams.

About the Author

Kate Fuglei is an actress, singer, and writer. She created a one-woman show, *Rachel Calof,* based on the memoir of a Jewish homesteader, and has performed it around America. It won Best Musical at the 2015 United Solo Festival in New York City. Kate has appeared in more than forty roles in episodic television and film, and she was in the First National Broadway tour of *Spring Awakening.* Based in Los Angeles, she has played leading roles in regional theaters across the country, among them Arena Stage, the Public Theater in New York City, and the La Jolla Playhouse. Two of Kate's short stories appeared in *SisterWriterEaters,* a book of essays about motherhood and food. Kate is the author of the Mentoris Project books *Fermi's Gifts: A Novel Based on the Life of Enrico Fermi, The Soul of a Child: A Novel Based on the Life of Maria Montessori,* and *The Embrace of Hope: A Novel Based on the Life of Frank Capra.* For more information about Kate, please visit katefuglei.com.

Building Wealth 101
How to Make Your Money Work for You
by Robert Barbera

Character is What Counts
A Novel Based on the Life of Vince Lombardi
by Jonathan Brown

Christopher Columbus: His Life and Discoveries
by Mario Di Giovanni

Dark Labyrinth
A Novel Based on the Life of Galileo Galilei
by Peter David Myers

Defying Danger
A Novel Based on the Life of Father Matteo Ricci
by Nicole Gregory

Desert Missionary
A Novel Based on the Life of Father Eusebio Kino
by Nicole Gregory

The Divine Proportions of Luca Pacioli
A Novel Based on the Life of Luca Pacioli
by W.A.W. Parker

Dreams of Discovery
A Novel Based on the Life of the Explorer John Cabot
by Jule Selbo

The Embrace of Hope
A Novel Based on the Life of Frank Capra
by Kate Fuglei

The Faithful
A Novel Based on the Life of Giuseppe Verdi
by Collin Mitchell

Fermi's Gifts
A Novel Based on the Life of Enrico Fermi
by Kate Fuglei

First Among Equals
A Novel Based on the Life of Cosimo de' Medici
by Francesco Massaccesi

The Flesh and the Spirit
A Novel Based on the Life of St. Augustine of Hippo
by Sharon Reiser and Ali A. Smith

God's Messenger
A Novel Based on the Life of Mother Frances X. Cabrini
by Nicole Gregory

Grace Notes
A Novel Based on the Life of Henry Mancini
by Stacia Raymond

Guido's Guiding Hand
A Novel Based on the Life of Guido d'Arezzo
by Kingsley Day

Harvesting the American Dream
A Novel Based on the Life of Ernest Gallo
by Karen Richardson

Humble Servant of Truth
A Novel Based on the Life of Thomas Aquinas
by Margaret O'Reilly

The Judicious Use of Intangibles
A Novel Based on the Life of Pietro Belluschi
by W.A.W. Parker

Leonardo's Secret
A Novel Based on the Life of Leonardo da Vinci
by Peter David Myers

Little by Little We Won
A Novel Based on the Life of Angela Bambace
by Peg A. Lamphier, PhD

The Making of a Prince
A Novel Based on the Life of Niccolò Machiavelli
by Maurizio Marmorstein

A Man of Action Saving Liberty
A Novel Based on the Life of Giuseppe Garibaldi
by Rosanne Welch, PhD

Marconi and His Muses
A Novel Based on the Life of Guglielmo Marconi
by Pamela Winfrey

No Person Above the Law
A Novel Based on the Life of Judge John J. Sirica
by Cynthia Cooper

The Pirate Prince of Genoa
A Novel Based on the Life of Admiral Andrea Doria
by Maurizio Marmorstein

Relentless Visionary: Alessandro Volta
by Michael Berick

Retire and Refire
Simple Financial Strategies to Navigate Your Best Years with Ease
by Robert Barbera

Ride Into the Sun
A Novel Based on the Life of Scipio Africanus
by Patric Verrone

Rita Levi-Montalcini
Pioneer & Ambassador of Science
by Francesca Valente

Saving the Republic
A Novel Based on the Life of Marcus Cicero
by Eric D. Martin

The Seven Senses of Italy
by Nicole Gregory

Sinner, Servant, Saint
A Novel Based on the Life of St. Francis of Assisi
by Margaret O'Reilly

Soldier, Diplomat, Archaeologist
A Novel Based on the Bold Life of Louis Palma di Cesnola
by Peg A. Lamphier, PhD

The Soul of a Child
A Novel Based on the Life of Maria Montessori
by Kate Fuglei

What a Woman Can Do
A Novel Based on the Life of Artemisia Gentileschi
by Peg A. Lamphier, PhD

The Witch of Agnesi
A Novel Based on the Life of Maria Agnesi
by Eric D. Martin

www.ingramcontent.com/pod-product-compliance
Lightning Source LLC
Chambersburg PA
CBHW060926190726
48286CB00002B/651